Dearest Readers,

In my Rogues of the Sea trilogy, three swashbuckling lords of
Regency England and their adventuresome ladies dare every-
thing for perfect love. The trilogy begins with *Swept Away By
a Kiss* (nominated for *RT Book Reviews'* Best First Historical
Romance) and continues with *Captured By a Rogue Lord* and
In the Arms of a Marquis, each a sizzling stand-alone romance.

I am thrilled now to offer you a taste of the series as an exclusive e-novella, *A Lady's Wish*, the love story of dashing war
hero Captain Nikolas Acton of the Royal Navy and the girl
he spent one glorious day with and could never forget. I hope
you enjoy Nik and Patricia's scandalously passionate reunion,
including cameo appearances of the heroes of my trilogy.

Happy romance and adventure!

Warmest wishes,
    Katharine

By Katharine Ashe
A Lady's Wish
Captured By a Rogue Lord
Swept Away By a Kiss

Coming Soon
In the Arms of a Marquis

A Lady's Wish

Katharine Ashe

AVONIMPULSE

Excerpt from *Captured By a Rogue Lord* copyright© 2011 by Katharine Brophy Dubois.

EPub Edition March 2011 ISBN: 978-0-06-209178-9

Print Edition ISBN: 978-0-06-212749-5

10 9 8 7 6 5 4 3

PROLOGUE

Two gentlemen stood upon the busy Portsmouth dock, the chill gray of February hanging over tall masts, broad decks and draft-drawn carts porting cargo to and fro. Pulled by a squat tug, a ship with furled sails moved slowly into berth along the quay, an elegant beauty, long as she was lovely, and powerful with fifty-six gunwales and a brace of iron pivots atop.

"A war hero, you say?" The younger gentleman, the Marquess of Doreé, dark of hair and eye, with bronzed skin and a quiet air, studied the vessel.

"They say," the Viscount of Ashford drawled, a hint of the Continent in his tone and garments. The latter were as costly as his friend's yet with the faintest suggestion of the dandy about them. His hair, short beneath a silk hat, glistened gold even in the gloom.

"Does he deserve the praise?"

"He does indeed." Lord Ashford glanced at the marquess's sober visage. "He is a good man. I believe he will accept our offer."

"No wealth to amuse him? No title to bind him?"

"Comfortable wealth won upon the sea against Boney.

Youngest son of a minor squire. Rather, too much time on his hands now that the war has ended." The viscount's amber gaze shifted to the officer at the vessel's helm, the man they had come to see. "Too much time in which to remember, and not enough activity to distract from those remembrances."

The marquess nodded, wise already despite his youth. "And if he accepts?"

"I will send him after Redstone, of course."

Lord Doreé turned his head and assessed the viscount carefully. Slowly a crease appeared in his cheek.

"I daresay," the viscount murmured.

"You will hire him to follow Redstone, but at a discreet distance, I trust?"

"Naturally. Don't wish to send the fellow to his death, after all."

The slight grin faded from Lord Doreé's mouth and his black eyes remained watchful. "Redstone will not be swayed to our cause. He is another sort of man altogether."

"I am not so certain of that." The viscount lifted a brow. "He steals from the rich to give to the poor, Ben."

"You may have played at being a pirate, Steven. But Redstone actually is one. He has killed more men than you and I have combined."

The viscount's eyes turned again to the man-of-war now slipping gracefully into her berth, the red, white and blue banner of empire snapping proudly atop the mizzenmast.

"And yet," he said quietly, "I will wager my fortune that our brave naval captain here has outstripped you, me, and Redstone together in that particular category. Desire for acknowledgment can lead a man to extraordinary lengths."

"Ah." The marquess scanned the deck for its captain. Though not yet above thirty, their quarry carried himself with authority, confidence in the set of his shoulders and the cast of his jaw. "When will you meet with him?"

"No time like the present." The viscount tapped his silver-tipped walking stick upon the planking in affected impatience. But they had waited four months already since the treaty that ended the war with France sent this sailor home to England after eight years upon the sea—this man they hoped to make an ally before he lost himself to the inevitable pleasures of society he had once left behind in favor of the theater of war.

Their work was noble, though unpopular. Yet here was a man who might be convinced to labor for them.

Upon deck the master of the 1500-ton warship called out orders to his men, his uniform of crisp blue and white favoring his broad frame.

"Welcome home, proud son of Britain," the viscount murmured. "Welcome home, Nikolas Acton."

CHAPTER ONE

"A true hero!" The matron fluttered her lacy kerchief beneath Nik's nose. Or perhaps beneath her own. It was a very large nose, like the nose of her daughter beside her. "My darling Tansy and I read of your commendation in the paper, Captain Acton," the mouth hidden beneath the cliff of the nose gushed. "I said to her, my dear Tansy, if a true hero is to attend the ball tonight, and such a handsome one, we must make his acquaintance if we should be so fortunate. And now we are so fortunate!"

"It is my honor, ma'am." Nik bowed and turned his attention upon the lady's daughter. The girl had a sweet smile and bright eyes. Appreciation for the nose could be learned.

But apparently the persistent sense within him that something was missing in the lady—*in all ladies*—could not be unlearned. Despite his efforts. For nearly a decade it had been the same. From smiling misses to stunning widows, he found himself searching for something he recognized. Something he had lost.

"Oh, no, Captain. It is our honor entirely!" The matron nudged her dear darling Tansy forward.

Nikolas set a gentle look upon the girl. "Would you care to dance, Miss Chapel?"

She nodded. They danced and he studied her smile. Chandeliers sparkled, violins trilled, flutes piped, guests laughed over glittering champagne, and his partner was a perfectly amiable young lady. His mother and sisters would be in alt. Home barely a month, and already he was seeking a wife.

"A wife," his mother had urged, "will help you establish yourself in society," as though Nik wished for none other than that.

"A wife," his sisters had giggled, "will spend all that gold you won at war," as though otherwise he might spend it all on carriages and cards.

"A wife," his father and elder brothers had glowered, "will finally thrash the fool boy out of you," as though eight years at war had not already seen to that.

A wife, Nik hoped, would force him to cease searching for that which he had not found in nine years.

"Captain Acton, you are staring at my mouth."

Not staring, precisely, merely lingering there in distraction.

"I beg your pardon. I am charmed. You have a lovely smile." A sweet, natural smile, in truth. But not the same. Never the same. He had only ever found remnants. The curve of a lower lip upon one lady. The glimmer of laughter in the eyes of another. The tilt of chin affected by a third. Hair, eyes, hands, shoulders, even the fabric of her gown. Everywhere he went, in every woman he encountered he saw memories of the girl he had known for a day, and lost just as swiftly.

"Oh." Miss Chapel dimpled. "I imagined a crumb stuck to my chin."

Nikolas chuckled then lowered his brow. "Absolutely not, madam. You appear pristine."

"Tiresomely so," she sighed, "although my mother would scream to hear me say it. But that spark lurking in your green eyes suggests you would rather that I appear other than I do."

"Never. And may I say, your *blue* eyes are quite as fine as your smile." But not cornflower blue.

"La, Captain. You will put me to the blush," she said disingenuously, but her dimples deepened, lessening the effect of the nose between them. "I am a painter, you see. I notice such things."

"Aha. Such things as?"

"The color of a person's eyes and the expression within them."

He smiled again. Yet nothing stirred within him but mild appreciation. It never did. Only that once.

He had been searching for that feeling—for that *woman*—ever since. Eight years ago the madness of searching in vain had driven him to war, escaping into the exclusive world of men to make himself halt his insanity. But now it was beginning again. A fortnight back in London and he looked for her everywhere, upon the street, in drawing rooms, in the lips and eyes and hair and hands of ladies he danced with in crowded ballrooms.

It was no way for a man to live. For a sailor, the master of a ship trained to hold his attention upon present concerns, it was lunacy. He'd thought his time at sea had broken him of the habit.

Apparently not.

"You are sad," his partner said. "And perhaps frustrated to be here tonight."

He released a short breath. "Miss Chapel, I fear my social graces have suffered in my absence from society. I beg your pardon for my poor behavior, for so it must be."

"Not at all, sir. I am simply overly observant. It is my curse."

The dance ended. He returned her to her mother but found he could bear no more of the lady's rhapsodic compliments or her daughter's perspicacious regard. He excused himself and walked to his club. No females could be found there to draw him into idiocy, or in the case of Miss Chapel, incivility. Nothing but gentlemen happy to eschew distracting feminine company for drink, game and conversation.

He scanned the General Chamber, tilting his hat to a pair of men he knew well—Braverton and Halloway, both white-haired officers at least twenty years his seniors upon the sea. But he was in no humor to talk with sailors tonight, especially not the happily married sort like these two. He required the company of men for whom women were merely momentary diversions, not lifetime commitments. Or obsessions.

He moved into the parlor and his shoulders relaxed. The answer to his prayer sat alone, perusing the paper. Wealthy, urbane, and as carelessly roguish as could be with the fairer sex, Alex Savege was precisely the man with whom Nik needed to spend time now.

He crossed the chamber, settled into the chair opposite his old school mate, and waved to a footman for a drink. The Earl of Savege lifted his attention from the paper in his perfectly manicured hand and a slow grin crossed his mouth.

"Ah. The hero returns to set himself down amongst mortal men. To what do I owe the honor of your much sought after company, Acton?"

"Enough of that at the ball I just escaped, Savage." Nik accepted a drink from the footman and tilted it to his mouth.

"Daresay," the earl murmured. "The very reason I tend to avoid balls."

Nik relaxed back into the soft leather chair. "How is your brother, Savege?"

"The same." Not even a flicker of interest showed upon the earl's handsome face. Three years earlier Nik had ferried Alex's twin to England as a favor. Coming off the battlefield in Spain, Aaron Savege had been half-dead. But perhaps Alex was simply better at hiding his thoughts than Nik. In school, Alex and Aaron had been close as brothers could be.

"And your family?" the earl asked. "I understand your sisters are taking society by storm."

"You do? Spending more time at balls than you care to admit?"

Savege grinned. "My mother and sister reside in my house here, of course. It is sometimes difficult to avoid hearing about that in which one has little interest."

"Do they—" He halted. Why had he come here and sought out this friend's company if he would broach such topics? The earl lifted a single brow in studied languor, just as he had when they used to drink themselves under the table in Cambridge. Now, however, rather more sobriety shadowed his gray eyes. That sobriety bade Nik continue despite his better judgment.

"Do they press you to find a wife, Alex?"

"What man's mother and sisters do not, Nik?"

"Point." Nik took a sip of his brandy, the same restlessness he had felt for two weeks unsettling him again. "Do you ever consider obliging them?"

"Why on earth should I?" This said with no inflection whatsoever. The rake was a rake, Nik understood well enough, because he did not in fact care.

Nik passed a hand across his face, surprised to find his jaw tight as well.

"Are you considering it?" The earl's tone remained perfectly smooth.

"Perhaps." Perhaps a wife would end the insanity of searching for her once and for all, searching for a girl who had left him waiting. A girl he had never deserved anyway. "Actually, I've had an offer from quite another direction that I am considering." He surprised himself in saying it aloud. He'd barely given it a thought since that day he stepped off his ship in Portsmouth and was met with a remarkable proposition from a gentleman he did not know.

He did not know Ashford, true. But amongst his fellow naval officers he'd heard rumors, odd rumors given the gentleman's foppish style and Continental drawl. Rumors that Lord Steven Ashford was not what he appeared to society. The tiny lines about his amber eyes and sun-touched hue of his skin suggested those rumors might be true—that Viscount Ashford occasionally captained his own ship, a ship dedicated to an intriguing purpose. Ashford's words to him that day proved it.

"An offer from a more appealing direction?" A wolfish gleam lit Alex's eyes.

Nik chuckled. "Quite another direction than that as well." He rubbed his jaw. "I had thought to purchase a house and settle upon land now that I have the wherewithal." Wherewithal he had lacked years ago when he met a girl to whom he would have given it all, a girl whose dress and air proclaimed her a lady of the highest breeding, no matter her sweetly candid manner with him.

"But?"

"But after a fortnight of balls, this offer tempts me more than I had imagined anything would tempt me to return to sea so soon."

His friend's eyes hooded.

Nik released a short laugh. "What am I saying? You wouldn't understand anything of the wish to be at sea or not, you libertine. No women to be found there."

"Indeed." The earl's fingertip traced the rim of his glass.

Nik's brow creased. "You've read about Redstone in the papers, I suspect. The pirate that likes to harry the ships of spoiled noblemen."

"I believe I have heard of him, yes."

"I've been offered the opportunity to go after him, but only to watch him." Ashford had been quite clear on that point. "Deuced peculiar mission, don't you think, to search out a pirate then sit like a duck on the water without apprehending him?"

"I'm afraid that I haven't an opinion on the matter one way or the other."

"Of course you haven't." Nik tried to shake off his discomfort with a laugh. But it clung. "But . . . I thought I might do it."

"Then no house or wife after all," Alex said smoothly. "This offer has not come from the Lord Commissioners of the Admiralty, I take it?"

"Private interest."

"Ah. A paying interest."

"A fellow would never agree to such a job otherwise." He

tried to grin. "Even a war hero with sacks of gold." Gold his father and brothers seemed to think merely proved his weak character, as though he had charmed French ships out of their treasures. But he had been a different man before he went to war, as careless and carefree as they believed.

Except concerning one girl.

A footman appeared by the table. "A letter for you, Captain."

Nik accepted the envelope from the silver tray. The hand was familiar. He and John Grace had corresponded since their school days. Throughout the war whenever Nik made land in Spain, Colonel "Jag" had found a way to meet him. Together they drank, chasing away with laughter the monotonies and horrors of the war they were fighting on sea and land.

"I shall leave you to your post." Savege unfolded from his chair with absolute grace, elegantly unscarred by any life other than pure hedonistic amusements. He could have laughed at Nik's ponderings. But he had not. Alex Savege might be a thorough rogue where women were concerned, but with gentlemen he was nothing but decent.

Nik stood and extended his hand. "It is good to see you again, Savege. Give my best to your brother, if you will."

"I will." His grip was firm and, oddly for a man of his indolent habits, slightly calloused. "Best of luck to you in coming to a decision. And if you should happen upon that nasty Redstone—" his eyes glittered "—beg him to have mercy upon my yacht, will you?"

Nik laughed. The earl released his hand and departed.

Nik settled back into his chair to open the envelope, and had to halt himself from reaching for the dirk in the sash he no longer wore. He did not miss the war, but he missed the weight of his rapier at his hip and pistol beneath his arm. An unarmed man was a man who could be wounded.

Are you capable of wounding a man?

I should hope not!

Excellent. Then I have nothing to fear.

He commanded a knife from a footman and slid the letter open. A single sheet of foolscap unfolded, another paper within it bound with brown string.

24 February 1816
Paris, France

Captain Nikolas Acton
c/o Farthings & Cholm Solicitors
Oxford Street
London, England

Dear Nik,

I trust you are well. I have been ordered by the general to set off at once for Calcutta and am pressed with last-minute preparations. I write in haste before departing with a commission for you. In truth, I trust only you to accomplish this task.

A close companion of my early years on the Peninsula—a gentleman I believe you met on one of your brief sojourns on land with us—discovered a treasure of great worth while there. He is no longer in a position to retrieve this treasure. Now, heading East, neither am I. Because of previous instructions left by my friend, however, the treasure will not

remain long in its present location in England. In short, it
could easily be lost.

I now put into your hands the map my friend fashioned.
You must retrieve the treasure before 15 March of this year.

Yours &c.

Colonel John "Jag" Pressley Grace

Nik unbound the map. He nearly laughed in relief. No
dotted line wended its way about the paper, no X marked
the spot. The "map" was rather a list of inns, posting houses,
villages, and rivers. All the places were familiar enough, running from London northwesterly toward Wales. He knew
that countryside well, indeed. He had spent a year scouring it,
searching for a girl. And he had begun his search in that very
village at the end of the list where Jag's friend had buried the
treasure.

He sipped his brandy slowly. Jag was an honest man. Nik
hadn't any doubt the treasure was above board.

His gaze shifted across the chamber. As a younger son
without prospects, profession, or wealth, he had not been welcome at clubs like this. Now he had the funds to match men
like Alex Savege at the gaming tables any day he wished.

He did not particularly wish it. And he did not wish a
wife, either. Not yet. Not until he finally rid himself of asinine
memories and foolish regrets. Ashford's offer was preferable to
enduring his six-month-long furlough in the state he'd spent
the past fortnight. The viscount had named an April 1 sailing
date. Nik would accept that offer. Until then this treasure hunt
would fill the time.

The fifteenth of March. Less than a fortnight. And the destination—the Shropshire Hills—where, on a sparkling May Day he had met a girl whose name he never learned. A girl he had laughingly called Isolde, after the heroine in the medieval play performed that day at the festival. Foolish devil-may-care youth that he had been, he'd told her to call him Tristan.

Tristan and Isolde, lovers who defeated all obstacles to be together until fate tore them apart.

Now, still he could not forget her. And again it was driving him mad.

He drew a long breath. He must move on with his life. Perhaps a visit to that place after so long would serve him as eight years upon the ocean had not. Perhaps seeing that tiny village again in the gray dripping rain of March rather than beneath the early summer sun would knock him into finally admitting that she had in fact been what he always feared.

Simply a dream.

Chapter Two

The prong would not budge.

Lady Patricia Morgan pressed her ribs into the edge of her worktable and squinted her eyes in the lamplight, as though such wiggling would make the tiny metal protrusion obey. Her breaths came tight and focused, her brow creased. But no matter how she prodded with the tip of the needle-thin pliers, the filigree of gold would not move across the tiny diamond's girdle.

"You wish to remain in that little divot of a flaw I did not see until it was too late, don't you?" she muttered to the recalcitrant prong. "But you will see, I will . . . Ah . . ." The pliers grasped just so, and she felt the certainty of it in her fingertips. "Oh . . ." Her breaths came quick and short, her teeth clenching. "Oo . . ."

"Tricky! A letter has arrived for you from Oliver's solicitors."

The pliers slipped, glancing off Patricia's thumb with a scrape of skin. Glaring at the delicate band of gold and diamonds fixed in the ring clamp, she reached for a cloth and enclosed her thumb in it.

"Thank you, Calanthia. You may leave it on the table." She glanced at her younger sister then returned her attention to the array of tools beside her. She hadn't any smaller pliers, and this particular ring would not bear anything larger.

"Didn't you receive a letter from them only last week?" Calanthia set the envelope at Patricia's elbow and plopped down in the soft chair beside her stool. There was not space in the chamber for more than the three pieces of furniture and her work chest. But she needn't any more space in which to make the rings. Only solitude.

Solitude was hard-won in the Morgan household.

"Your nephew's estate requires a great deal of managing." She ran her fingertips through her tools, trusting. They often found what they needed best when she allowed them to feel their way naturally. "How happy I might have been as a tinker's daughter."

"Don't say that near the dowager. She despises tinkers." Calanthia twirled a short strand of shimmering carroty hair between her fingers. "She despises all tradesmen. A man from the butcher's came around the other day and she nearly took a strap to him, though I haven't any idea what the poor fellow could have said to send her flying into the boughs like that."

That they had not paid their bills in a month and he would cease delivering to the stylish London townhouse of young Sir John Morgan if his mother would not deliver some coin in return.

"My mother-in-law is of a sensitive nature." Her fingers paused. The Swiss file! She would shave the nasty little prong into submission.

"Aren't you going to open it?"

"Not now, dear." She set the file to the ring. It would be tricky . . . "And please, Callie, do not let Lady Morgan hear you calling me that again. She believes it is beneath me."

"But you don't. May I open it?"

"Be my guest." It was probably time Calanthia understood the straits in which Patricia's sons were now. Poor handling of Oliver's funds by his former solicitors while he served in Spain had depleted the estate. Only now, after three and a half years of careful planning and the dedicated work of a new steward, was it returning slowly to order.

A pinch established itself between her shoulders and worked its way up her neck.

She had hoped to remain in London until funds would come from the countryside. But this news of the butcher boded ill. They must soon remove again to the remote estate upon which Oliver had sequestered her for five years, until he perished in Spain and she had been free to move to London as she had long desired.

She glanced at Calanthia unfolding the pages and her heart caught. Her energetic young sister filled the house with good spirit. But Patricia could not afford to bring her out into society as she deserved. Callie must go live with their brother, Timothy, and his wife. She could not very well throw out Oliver's nasty mother or dear old maiden aunt, after all.

She returned her attention to the ring. The diamonds were barely chips. But they were all she could afford.

It would be the last one. This she must also give up, her single passion other than her sons. Her only passions since she had relinquished any hope of ever experiencing any other sort of passion. The sort of passion of which she had once dreamed.

The pinch became a pain.

"Mama! Mama! Ramsay has bit me again!"

Two small tempests exploded into the room, carrot-headed like their aunt and entirely unlike Patricia's brown hair, knocking her table and sending her tools flying.

"I did not! John is lying!"

"I am not." Her eldest son, six and full of the consequence due a baronet and in perfect imitation of the father he had barely known, drew himself up to his slender height and lifted his chin. "Mama, I will not have this insub— insubnordention in my house. You must send Ramsay off to school at once."

"Beast!" Ramsay banded his little arms about her waist and buried his face in her smock.

Setting down the file, she stroked her hand over her younger son's soft curls and took a thoughtful breath, the ache in her head intensifying. She looked into her elder son's pale eyes and spoke softly.

"John, I believe you may find it more effective to address insubordination with mercy and education about right behavior rather than threats of exile." She bent to speak over Ramsay's head. "And you, Ramsay, will discover that if you cease attacking your brother with your teeth he will love you more greatly and not wish to see you gone."

"But he—" came muffled from her waist. "He said that— that tall man with the red waistcoat was to be our new papa, and I do not like that man."

"Hm. I see." Patricia returned her gaze to her eldest. "John, why did you tell your brother that?"

"Grandmamma said it. She said a lady with two sons must have a husband and that Lord Perth is to be our new papa."

Pain leapt right over Patricia's brow and down behind her eyes.

"Well, your grandmother likes Lord Perth, that is true. But I have no plans for him to become your new papa. If I should even begin considering it, however, I will consult with you first." She kissed Ramsay's curls. "Will that suit you?"

He lifted his head, his cheeks ruddy and damp. "Yes, Mama. Thank you, Mama."

"And you, John?"

"Yes, Mama. I beg your pardon for telling an untruth." But his face was too severe, too serious for a boy of six. He wished for a father. He had told Patricia this many times, from nearly the moment he could speak. Uncle Timothy was not enough, he once confided. He wished for a papa of his own.

"Now then, Nurse must be looking for you to put you to bed. I shall be up in a trice to tuck you in." She kissed her younger son on the top of his head and stroked her fingertips along John's cheek. The boys turned and stumbled through a quintet of fat little tawny dogs pushing into Patricia's workroom. Her mother-in-law appeared where her sons had been. Arrayed in bronze taffeta with a spray of black feathers jutting from a bandeau, with yet another pug in her arms, the Dowager Lady Morgan took in the scene with a pinched nose.

"You missed another exemplary musical fete, daughter. And what have you accomplished in its stead?" She flicked a hand toward the tools scattered upon the floor. "Trinkets for worthless tarts."

"They are not trinkets, Mother." She bent to retrieve the tools. "They are wedding rings, and the girls who receive them through the foundling hospital are not tarts. They are brides."

Poor brides. But poverty was something the Dowager Lady Morgan would never understand. Even were Patricia to show her the pile of bills upon her escritoire, her mother-in-law would sniff and say that ladies did not pay bills.

Oliver had said the same thing in his letters from Spain. And his worthless solicitors had taken advantage of that. Now, of course, she simply *could not* pay bills.

"Was there something you wished, Mother?" She picked up the last of her tools, scratched a pug beneath its tiny ear, then began lining up the pliers neatly.

"Lord Perth has suggested to me that if you were to show him more encouragement he would not be adverse to making you an offer."

Patricia pivoted on her stool. "He suggested that to you? How remarkable."

"I told him he should not look for encouragement from a lady, only modesty. But he seems uncertain of your intentions." She pursed her thin lips. "What are they, Patricia? To leave your sons fatherless indefinitely?"

She swallowed tightly. "My intentions are not Lord Perth's particular business."

"You are an ungrateful girl. I always told my son that."

Patricia swiveled back to face her work, her palms damp. "Your son knew that well enough all on his own." A chubby little dog bumped against her ankle and it felt far too comforting, warm and affectionate and alive. "Is that all, Mother? I have quite a bit of work left to finish tonight."

The dowager sniffed pointedly, fingers stroking the pug in her grasp. "Ladies do not work."

Patricia's megrim spiraled. "This lady does." She plucked

up the pliers. "Good night, Mother. Sleep well."

The rustle of fabric and pattering of twenty little paws signaled the dowager's departure. Patricia set the pliers to the diamond anew, her chest and throat tight. But it was no use. Her hands were no longer steady.

Out of financial necessity she would cease this work she loved and her mother-in-law would declare victory. She would send Calanthia to their brother's house and lose the last ray of unrelenting sunshine in her life. She would move the rest of her family to the country where their company would be limited, with only sweet senile Aunt Elsbeth to defray the effects of the dowager's daily disparagements. She would do it all if she must.

But she would not marry a man she did not love. Not again. Not even for the sake of her sons. She had done so once to suit her family. She had long since promised herself she would never do so again.

Instead, inside her where she was most wicked, another idea sparked. An idea she had dreamt for months but hadn't had the courage to think through entirely. A shameful idea that made her heart race and head dizzy to truly consider now.

She would have an affair. She would experience passion. *With a man.*

The very thought of it swept the megrim quite away.

Married ladies occasionally talked, and Patricia had come to understand that it was possible for a lady to feel more than pain or boredom during the marriage act. Lately her mind had fixed upon that tantalizing notion until she was frantic for a taste of that something else. Perhaps it was the desperate straits she had fallen into, or the sameness of her life every day despite her troubles.

She needed a holiday. She needed *passion*. She wanted laughter and desire and to feel freely alive again. She certainly would not feel it with Lord Henry Perth, a fine gentleman in his stiff, stoic English sobriety. Just like Oliver. But if she must wed again eventually, would it be so wrong to live a little—for even a day, *a night*—before that?

She breathed a silent sigh.

It was pure fantasy, of course. In London where she lived the portrait existence of a proper widow, if she were found out it could be disastrous. She had her sons to consider, and Callie whose introduction into society the following year must not be tainted by gossip.

Perhaps even more to the point, true ladies did not indulge in fits of passion or even excessive affection. Her mother had taught her that, and Oliver reinforced it. In those first months of marriage she had been so unhappy. But after that, even when she tried to give him warmth, all he had ever wanted of her was one thing, and even that he had done without feeling. No warmth at all. No passion. Finally she had given up trying. When he purchased a commission and headed off to war, they had both known why.

But all men were not like Oliver. Some were passionate. She had kissed a man of that sort once. On one perfect day she had tasted heaven.

She positioned the pliers at the diamond's girdle anew. Her hands were steady again, her breathing even. Merely indulging in thoughts of her fantasy calmed her.

"Tricky?" From her place sunk in the chair, Calanthia's voice was unusually soft.

"What is it, dear?"

"This is not a letter from Oliver's solicitor." She lifted a round gaze. "It is a letter from Oliver himself."

Patricia's hands stilled upon her tool.

"From Oliver *Morgan*? My husband?"

"Read it."

A top sheet of engraved stationery from Oliver's solicitor included one line only: *1 March 1816. Dear Lady Morgan, I am instructed to deliver this to you at this time. Yours &c., Harold Glover.* The other page was written in Oliver's familiar, passionless script, but peculiarly thin and uneven. It was dated three days after the Battle of Salamanca in which he was wounded. The day before his death.

25 July 1812
Salamanca, Spain

Lady Patricia Ramsay Morgan
Lowescroft
Bradford, England

My dear wife,

You are no doubt wondering what I must say to you at this final moment. I have never been demonstrative, and rest assured I will not become so now upon the eve of my death. For I am quite certain that I shall die shortly. My wound is grave and the doctors are not optimistic.

Before I leave you to this present world a widow, however, I must enjoin upon you a final task. I ask it of you for the sake of our sons to whom I have been a poor father. I offer one caveat before I continue: if you are once again wed—and more

happily this time, I pray—do not read this letter. Rather,
throw it into the grate and allow the flames to consume it. For
in this case I have no more authority over you, and your new
husband has all that I have already lost. But if you are not yet
wed again, I beg of you, do as I request. It is a last wish from
a husband who should have been a better one to you but who
knew not how.

Not long ago I caused to have buried in the ground in
England an object of great value. Its retrieval will ensure our
sons' future happiness. Recall the home of your distant cousins
at which we became betrothed. You must go there to retrieve
the object, but you must do so within a fortnight of receiving
this letter.

I leave you now with a final word, one of gratitude. You
have been an excellent mother to our children. You were—
despite all—an exemplary wife to me. I wish you every
happiness and God's blessings.

> *Yours,*
> *Oliver Christopher Morgan, III*

Patricia sat mute, her eyes prickling.

"Tricky? Are you all right?"

She blinked, sweeping her hand across her eyes and dashing away a pair of tears.

"Yes. Quite all right."

"You *are*?"

She nodded, a little surprised at the truth of her words.
His final thanks and blessing was more than she had ever had
from him in life. It was far too late and far too little, of course.
But she had learned quite early in their marriage that he had

not been capable of expressing more. She no longer faulted him for it.

And now she could thank him for the opportunity he afforded her.

She folded up the pages and tucked them in her pocket. "I will ask Aunt Elsbeth to accompany me."

Her sister gaped. "Will you do it, then?"

"Of course. Why shouldn't I?"

"But—" Callie sat forward. "But, Tricky, you haven't any idea what he is sending you *to*. And for goodness sake it could be long gone by now!"

She tilted her head. "For a girl of usually high spirits, you are reacting to this rather oddly."

"I suppose I am simply flabbergasted. I have never received a letter from a dead husband I did not like above half. I cannot imagine how you must feel right now."

"I feel fine." Better than fine. Tingling, in fact. She glanced at her work. She could not finish it tonight. Now she must pack for her journey. She stood up and untied her apron.

Callie leapt out of her chair. "I will go with you."

Patricia's brow creased. If she were going to do what she was considering, she could not very well have her seventeen-year-old sister in tow.

"You must remain here to comfort John and Ramsay in my brief absence."

"They will have Nurse, and John's tutor, and of course their horrid grandmother. And I am the only person who knows how to rub Aunt Elsbeth's feet when they get the cramps. If you are going to take her as chaperone, you must take me too."

"Hm." She considered her sister's bright eyes, bluer than

her own and full of animation. Once she had been that same age, and she had met a man who made her head spin and heart stop. Calanthia did not know that, of course; Patricia had only ever told her diary of it. But after bearing the dowager's company for nearly four years, her sister deserved a holiday too.

"All right."

"Oh, Tricky, you are tremendous!" She threw her arms about her and squeezed. Patricia held the embrace, savoring the closeness.

Calanthia hopped to the door. "I am off to pack. Oh, I simply cannot wait to see Lady Morgan's face pinch up like a prune when she hears about this!" She dashed from the chamber.

Patricia withdrew the letter and opened it again. The journey would require several days, just as it had nine years ago in the opposite direction—that journey commenced on the same day Oliver had asked her to be his bride, a full day after he had already signed the betrothal contract with her father.

But this time Patricia was not betrothed. And she was not to be married to one man while her heart longed for another. Upon this journey, she would not be weeping tears that for the next months seemed to have no end except when she hid them from her new husband.

On this journey she would be free. A respectable widow. A woman with a family, barely a penny in her purse, and an aching desire for an experience that would bring her to life again for a moment. Upon the road, a lady was bound to encounter at least one man willing to oblige her fantasy. A man to offer her a taste of passion for a single night, passion that would rekindle feelings she had only ever felt once.

This time, however, if she happened to come across a handsome gentleman who made her feel alive from the inside out, she would learn his name before he disappeared forever.

CHAPTER THREE

"'**T**is only a strain, mum."

Rain fell in a mizzling shroud across the muddy highway and dripped off the brim of Patricia's bonnet. Only two of the carriage horses still rested in their traces. The coachman had detached the leaders to walk them about. The left leader limped dramatically.

Patricia wrinkled her brow. "Only a strain?"

"Aye, mum. He'll be better in a jiffy, I 'spect."

"What is a *jiffy* precisely in this case, Carr?"

"Two days. P'raps three if I put a poultice on it right quick. I'll know better in the morning, mum."

She looked up the road, then in the opposite direction. Little could be seen but shadows of trees and the edges of fields hemmed in by stone fences. But according to Oliver's letter, there should be an inn close by.

"Then we will drive to the nearest posting house and change them out before continuing," she said bracingly.

"Could, mum." Carr nodded. "If he could do it."

"The horse is no longer able to pull the carriage?"

Carr shook his head and scratched beneath the brim of his

high-crown hat. "'Fraid not, mum. Less you'd like him good for naught else again."

"No, of course not." She glanced at the complex harnessing. "Can you tie him behind and drive the others until we reach the posting house?"

"No, mum." He looked chagrined. "Begging your pardon."

"Hm." She took a deep breath and released it upon a puff. "Then we must simply wait for help to happen by."

"I could ride on ahead?" He looked doubtful.

"No. That would leave us quite unprotected. We will wait it out." She dusted the rain from her cloak and climbed back into the carriage. Within, Callie's blue eyes sparkled with curiosity and Aunt Elsbeth's prominent gray orbs looked pleasantly smudgy as usual.

"The lead horse has suffered a strained fetlock." She patted Oliver's maiden aunt's hand. "But you needn't worry. Help will be along shortly and we will be on our way to a nice cozy inn before we know it."

"Dear me, Patricia." Aunt Elsbeth's thin, tripping tones were somewhat musical. "You do say the oddest things."

She laughed. "But it is true, Aunt Elsbeth."

"I daresay that farm will do well enough for the afternoon." The elderly lady bobbed her head, a tangled mass of silk flowers jiggling in reds, blues and yellows atop her bonnet, crinkles at the edges of her mouth.

Patricia peered out the window. "Did you see a farm, then?"

"Oh, no, my dear. Not for months now."

Patricia flicked her gaze to her sister. Calanthia grinned and rolled her bright eyes, then tucked her hand in Aunt Elsbeth's elbow.

"Auntie, tell us at what distance we sit now from that farm, if you will."

"We are a quarter mile past it, I should say."

Callie cuddled closer to the elderly lady. "And what are they serving for dinner today at the farm?"

"Mutton stew."

"There, Tricky. We shall have mutton stew in short order. Shall we walk? Although it would be a great deal more diverting to remain here and be accosted by a highwayman, I suspect. I have heard such bandits are excessively roguish."

Patricia tried not to smile. Aunt Elsbeth would meander, and Callie would play, just as they did at home in London. They seemed content enough, despite the cold creeping through gloves and shoes.

"Mum," Carr called from without. "Rider's coming along."

She opened the door and poked her head out.

"Does it look like a highwayman, Tricky?"

"I am not perfectly familiar with the physical attributes of highwaymen, sister, but I shall ask him. If he replies in the affirmative I will inform you directly."

"Splendid!"

The rider neared. Unfortunately for Calanthia, he looked unexceptionably like a gentleman, in an elegant caped greatcoat and brimmed hat, a saddle pack behind him. His handsome horse loped along the muddy road with ease. Patricia set her foot upon the step.

"Ask him about the farm," Callie chirped.

Patricia grinned and climbed out into the drizzle.

"He has slowed his horse to a walk, Auntie." Callie peeked out and narrated for Aunt Elsbeth within. "Oh, bother. He is dismounting. That is certainly not the action of a bandit. He is very tall and walks with great confidence, but he brandishes no pistol. How disappointing."

"Calanthia," Patricia whispered, "be still." She adopted a gracious smile and turned to the gentleman walking toward the carriage. "Good day, sir. I wonder if we might prevail upon you to . . ."

She got no further.

He halted as her speech did, four yards away.

Her breathing stopped.

His eyes widened for an instant. Green eyes. She knew this even across the space between them now.

She knew it from her memory.

It was *he*. Tristan. After nine years.

But she must be wrong. This man's face was not the same as in her memory. In the pale light of the misty day his skin appeared tanned. A firm jaw and smooth cheeks flanked not smiling lips and a long straight nose, but the hard line of a mouth and a nose at least once broken.

His lips parted slightly, as though he might speak. Then he removed his hat and bowed with military precision. His hair was as she remembered it, nearly black although very short. He straightened and replaced the hat, obscuring in shadow once more the dark, rich emeralds that had once gazed at her with thorough longing.

"Good day, madam. May I be of assistance?"

Patricia could not find her voice. *His* was the same, only altered slightly, deepened by the breadth of his chest which seemed wider. His shoulders as well. The years had rendered the youth a man.

"Tricky," her sister whispered and poked her in the kidneys.

Patricia knew not how she managed to curtsy. Her breaths would not return to her compressed chest and her entire body felt shaky. She had not until this moment realized that she never expected to see him again. For months she had dreamed. For years she had wondered. But she never truly believed she would, convincing herself that her young, hungry imagination had invented him.

But England was not such a large place after all. She had been a fool.

"Thank you, sir." Her voice sounded odd and stiff, the rain dulling sounds all about. "We have horse trouble and cannot continue to the inn ahead."

"There is a farm not a quarter mile behind," he said without hesitation, winning a titter from within the carriage. "I will ride back and return with an alternate conveyance. Does your coachman carry a pistol?"

There was no gracious solicitation here, no hint of recognition beyond that first brief pause. Only attention to necessity.

"I believe so. Carr?"

"Yes, mum." Carr pulled aside his coat to reveal the butt of a weapon.

"See that you use it if necessary." He spoke with complete authority, as though accustomed to giving orders. He turned and remounted. "I will return shortly." He bowed from the saddle, circled his horse about and with a smacking of hooves in mud, set off at a canter.

Patricia pressed a hand to her chest, to force breath into her lungs or to still her pounding heart, she hardly knew.

Tristan. The man over whom she had cried a thousand

tears. Come to life. Appearing upon a rainy road in the middle
of nowhere.

"He has gone to fetch us another carriage, Auntie," she
heard Calanthia say cheerily. "And you will not believe it
when you see him—he is *very* handsome. I daresay we should
be stranded upon the road more often if such gentlemen will
appear to rescue us."

There was no carriage to be found at the farm, of course, only
a wagon without covering. But it must suffice. Afternoon was
fast waning and the rain would darken the road before the sun
set. So it was on land, just as on the sea.

Nik commandeered the wagon and the farmer to drive it.
In a lengthy exposition the farmer explained his eldest son's
inability to drive now on account of an injury involving a bale
of hay, a pitchfork, an overly feisty cow, and a pretty dairymaid.

"Females," the farmer spat. "Always a female, ain't it, sir?"

Always a female, indeed.

Nik had sailors as loquacious as the farmer aboard his ship;
he did not mind the chatter. Indeed, he welcomed it. Anything
to force his mind into a semblance of order resembling the
order that had reigned in his life for eight years since he ran
away to the Navy because of a woman. The woman stranded
upon the road before him now.

*You must join the Navy and become a great ship captain! You
will be the scourge of Napoleon's fleet.*

She was entirely altered. Her cheeks, once rosy as a ripe
peach and dimpled, were now hollowed and pale, rendering her
chin more angled and casting shadows beneath her eyes. Her
hair, then as multifaceted as autumn leaves and shining in the

sunlight as it slipped out of its ribbons, now disappeared in a tight knot beneath her sober bonnet. And her mouth, lips he remembered as the sweetest, softest dusky rose, and full enough to drive a man mad imagining them upon him . . .

She had smiled until she recognized him. Then her smooth cheeks and sensuous lips had gone pale as a specter's.

If Nik needed any sign to confirm that she remembered him and had no desire to meet him again, he now had that sign. His chest felt tight and he felt like a reckless, uncertain youth still. A war hero brought down finally by a woman's blank stare.

But it was merely confirmation of what he had suspected even then.

From the moment he had first caught a glimpse of her that morning, her hair sparkling in the early summer sunshine and elegant dress caressing her young curves, he'd known he was not good enough for her. He had never been good enough for anything, as his father and elder brothers never hesitated to remind him. Never intelligent enough, never disciplined enough, never talented enough to merit praise or even much attention other than censure. He was nothing more than a careless wastrel. That she had laughed and smiled and allowed him to kiss her had not changed that, no matter how he wished otherwise. By the end of that golden day he had determined that in order to win her he would make something of himself. It would be that simple.

But she had not met him the following morning as planned, and she could not be found. So he had gone to war to make something else entirely of himself.

He spurred his mount onward. The carriage appeared in the gray ahead, the horses sodden in their traces. After a full day in the saddle, Nik was tired and sore. But if Jag's instructions and his own memory were correct, the route offered an inn not five miles distant. With the wagon, it might be reached before nightfall.

She came out of the carriage and peered down the road behind him.

"Ah. What good fortune." She clasped gloved hands before her. She was still slender, the curve of her shoulders and rise of her breasts barely discernable beneath her cloak. "Thank you, sir."

"A wagon?" A young lady poked her bright head through the doorway. "How singular!"

He bowed. "I fear the options were limited, ma'am. It was either this or the donkey cart. I dared to decide for you."

The girl giggled, dimpling up in a manner so familiar—so gut grabbingly familiar, so emblazoned in his memory—he knew she must be a relation. He shifted his gaze to the lady he had not been able to forget in nine years, then wished he had not.

Her blue eyes—eyes he had lost himself in once before—were trained upon him, thick-lashed and wide, cornflowers set in a face too lovely to be real. Lovely, not because he remembered it glowing with youthful innocence and desire. Not because that face had not changed, for it had. But because now, as then when he had first seen her in the crowd at the festival and lost his breath, she was to him the most beautiful thing he had ever beheld.

He could not deny it to himself. He did not even wish to.

"It will do splendidly, of course," she only said. "Carr, it will be dark within an hour. Will you be comfortable remaining here with the carriage and horses until help can be sent back?"

"'Course, mum. Don't you be worrying on me." He nodded her along then began unstrapping the luggage from the top of the vehicle.

Nik extended his hand for the girl inside and she jumped down lightly.

"This is a most provident adventure!"

"Mishaps upon highways in the rain and mud cannot be considered anything but, ma'am."

"You are quizzing and we are hardly known to one another!" Her eyes twinkled. "Oh, Tricky, I am quite glad he was not a highwayman after all. You are not, are you, sir?"

"Not for years now."

"Then I am terribly disappointed we did not encounter you earlier in life." She giggled, all silly girlish glee. Not like that other girl he remembered as though it were yesterday. That girl had laughed freely, but with quiet grace. Her eyes had sparkled but her lashes allowed only a glimmer of that joy to shine forth. She had been fervent yet modest, and she had not directly told him her feelings that day, an omission which he noted far too late.

She stood now silent, watching them.

An elderly lady appeared in the door and he assisted her down.

"Young man, you must see to that scar now or it will pain you in old age." She patted his shoulder, released him, and wobbled toward the wagon.

The girl's eyes danced. Nik lifted a brow. She stifled another giggle. The farmer tugged his cap and Nik assisted the elderly lady onto the seat. With a wide grin the girl climbed over the low rear slat into the back of the cart.

"I have not ridden in the back of a wagon for years," she exclaimed in pleasure, arranging her skirts across the sodden hay.

He turned his attention to the lady at his side. "I regret that you must ride in one now."

A wagon is not a suitable conveyance for a lady.

He offered his hand. She did not look at him, but placed her gloved fingers upon his palm, and after nine years he touched her again.

It was not the heart-stopping madness he had experienced when on a sparkling May Day she had entwined her fingers with his and the sweet, soft caress of her skin set him afire. This touch—deliberate and steady—gave nothing. No uncertainty. No familiarity. No suggestion that she might find this meeting awkward, confusing or daunting. While to him the very weight and shape of her fingers took his breath.

She stepped on to the straw and released him, then tucked her gown neatly about her and directed her gaze forward.

He went to his horse, his chest tight. He had spent years on the sea fighting men cowardly and brazen, greedy and vicious. In service to the Crown he had fought battles worthy of nightmares. He had held the helm steady at twenty-five knots against storms that would break a madman, his heart in his throat, praying for redemption. But he had never felt like a fool until now.

For years he had worshipped the dream of a woman who no longer existed. Quite possibly, she never had.

Chapter Four

He rode alongside the wagon, darkly handsome and silent as the evening fell around them and the road grew dimmer. The wagon jolted under Patricia's behind, her hands raw where she clutched the edge. Calanthia maintained a steady stream of conversation with the talkative farmer, Aunt Elsbeth inserting morsels of absurdities throughout. But Patricia could not enjoy it.

How could her blood tingle and yet she felt as though she were dying inside, both at once? He had taken her hand and her entire universe halted.

It was *he*. Still she could not believe it, possibly because he was behaving as though they had never met. As though their day together had not been the most wonderful of her life. Followed directly by the most heartbreaking.

Lights appeared ahead, and the shadows of buildings clustered about a yard. The wagon rumbled to a halt before the inn, a mostly stone structure of two stories. Calanthia took their escort's hand to descend. Sore and stiff, Patricia hurried clumsily off the back of the wagon before he could assist her. She could not bear touching him again so perfunctorily, not remembering how they had once touched in quite another manner.

"I hope the fire is blazing," Calanthia said cheerily. "I am chilled to the bone."

Inside, the sounds of a busy taproom came from beyond the foyer. A robust, salt-and-pepper-haired man wearing an apron appeared in the doorway.

"How may I be of service to you, sir?"

"I am Acton. My man came ahead of me today to arrange accommodation."

The innkeeper bowed with a sweep of his hand. "Welcome, Captain Acton! We are honored to have the Navy's finest here at the Trout and Pony."

Patricia gaped.

Captain Acton? The naval officer praised for his victories so often during the war that not a person in England did not know of his fame?

"You must see to these ladies first," he instructed the innkeeper. "They have had a time of it upon the road with an injured carriage horse and require private quarters as well as a parlor for dinner and breakfast."

"I wish I could oblige, Captain." The innkeeper was all obsequious regret. "But we have only one parlor and your man here—" He gestured to a weathered, bowlegged man shuffling into the foyer "—has already hired it for you."

"I have no need of it. It shall be theirs."

"Oh, no, sir. Captain." Words stumbled from Patricia's tied tongue. "You must not relinquish it for us."

"Taproom's not fit for ladies," his manservant scowled. "Cap'n ain't supped with fellows so low going on five years."

"That is not precisely true, Rum. I have supped with you."

Calanthia giggled.

"I regret your man has it right." The innkeeper shook his head. "Filled to the brim with laborers tonight, Captain."

Captain Acton turned to her. "I would not leave you to such company and suffer the chastisement of both Mr. Rum and our host." His green eyes sparkled, so like the young man nine years ago it grabbed Patricia's breath.

A smile tugged at her lips. "Is that the only reason?"

He lifted a curious brow. "Of course."

"Then you must accept our invitation to dinner." Her fingers plucked at her cloak, a habit of nerves. His gaze upon her was far too steady and inside she was tangled and regretful and anticipatory at once. Thoroughly confused. In all her fantastical imagined scenarios of how he had been busy enjoying life carelessly making love to women he briefly encountered whilst she moldered away in a remote corner of England trapped there by her husband, she had never, *never* imagined him a famous sea captain. Never.

I can sail fairly well. And I can, apparently, fall in love with a lady whose name I do not know within the course of a few short hours.

"Oh, yes, Captain." Callie beamed. "You must join us for dinner."

"Roast capons and turnips." Aunt Elsbeth's bonnet flowers bounced. "And leek pie."

Callie laughed. "Leek pie, Auntie?"

"Been sneaking in the kitchen a'times, I'll wager." Mr. Rum scratched behind his ear, a bushy brow raised.

"I beg your pardon. My aunt does not sneak about kitchens." Callie's voice censured, but her eyes twinkled. "She is simply prescient."

"Well I dunno what's that, miss." He eyed Aunt Elsbeth. "But she's got the lay o what's in the galley."

"Pray join us, Captain," Patricia said quietly. "I shall not hear differently."

He bowed to her. He could hardly do otherwise with all three of them and his manservant insisting. But she did not think he liked it. His brow was taut.

The innkeeper finally turned to her.

"And who, ma'am, may I be welcoming with the captain here?"

"I am Lady Morgan." She looked at the war hero she had known for a single day as a carefree, teasing youth, and said, "Captain Acton, may I present to you my sister, Miss Ramsay? This is Miss Haye, my husband's aunt." She did not know why those last words should be so difficult to say. She was no longer wed now, after all. As she had not been on the day she met him.

"I am honored to be favored with such company." He bowed again. "I beg you to excuse me while Mr. Rum and I see to your cattle and vehicle."

"You needn't, sir. Our coachman will."

"Not alone, he cannot." He turned and without another word went out of the inn.

Patricia stared into the cheval glass on the parlor wall at a face she barely recognized. She had packed all her prettiest traveling dresses, including a light muslin she liked, in the naïve, heady hopes of encountering a gentleman upon the journey who might admire her. But she had not given a thought to her face or hair. She had not imagined she might encounter a gentleman who had known her nine years ago when the bloom still glowed in her cheek and she hadn't gray circles beneath her eyes from lack of sleep and too many cares.

She never imagined encountering him at all.

"Is this not the most splendid inn?" Calanthia danced into the parlor with a swirl of skirts. "The chambers are all done up in chintz and lace pillows, so there must be a very busy lady innkeeper."

"Callie, where is Aunt Elsbeth?"

"Mr. Rum seems to be taking her to task for something she said concerning Noah's Ark. I passed them in the corridor quarreling."

"Calanthia." Patricia started for the door. "You cannot simply leave her conversing in private with a man of whom we know nothing."

"But Captain Acton is so splendid, I cannot imagine his manservant would be anything but splendid as well. And apparently he is the captain's cabin steward. Sailors are so honorable."

Patricia shook her head and reached for the doorknob. The panel swung open and she came face-to-face with the man she had dreamt about on her wedding night. His gaze swept over her features, then her hair. She lifted a hand to a curl that would not be restrained by pins no matter how she tried. He followed the action.

"What a wonderful place this is, don't you agree, Captain?" Calanthia opened a small wooden casket on the mantle. "Why, look! A treasure chest. And it is even filled with tiny faux gold doubloons. How delightful. John and Ramsay would adore it, wouldn't they, Tricky?"

"I suspect they would," she murmured.

"I should wonder at a treasure chest so far from the coast," he said over her shoulder. But she was standing in his way of entering the room, of course, staring at him as though he were not real. She backed up a step. He moved into the chamber and to Calanthia.

"You must certainly know of such things, Captain." Callie's fingertips ruffled through the coins then she replaced the box. "We have heard of your great victories during the war. What brings you now so far from your ship?"

"Calanthia," Patricia whispered.

He glanced at her. "I do not mind the question. I am on a mission on behalf of a friend, Miss Ramsay. In pursuit of a hidden treasure, in fact."

"How diverting!" She clapped her hands. "What sort of treasure?"

"I haven't an idea. What sort of a treasure do you wish it to be?" He smiled.

Patricia's knees went to jelly. But her sister seemed unaffected by this display of masculine perfection.

"What sort? Goodness me, if I could choose I would have it be a chest filled to the brim with diamonds, rubies, sapphires, and emeralds."

"Aha, gems." His amusement was all for Calanthia. "A lady's fondest wish."

"Not every lady's." The words passed through Patricia's lips before she could halt them. But her fondest wish for years had been him.

Calanthia laughed. "But, Tricky, with such a treasure you could make wedding rings for hundreds of poor girls."

He turned to her with a mildly curious regard, hands folded behind his back, bearing erect. "Wedding rings?"

"My sister you see," Calanthia supplied, "is an amateur jeweler. A remarkably fine one. She makes wedding rings for girls in London whose grooms cannot afford to supply rings themselves."

"How admirable of you, Lady Morgan."

His voice, deep and slightly rough, made her weak as it had nine years ago. He had spoken to her that day, so few words to begin, and like a puppy hungering for a biscuit, she had followed him. And she had believed his words.

She could not meet his gaze. "Thank you, sir." She turned to the door as Aunt Elsbeth, Mr. Rum, and a serving girl bearing a tray laden with dishes entered.

"Rain's settling in tonight, Cap'n." Mr. Rum began distributing dishes and serving them. "Travelin'll be poor tomorrow."

"But I daresay you've had plenty of poor weather at sea, haven't you?" Calanthia plucked a slice of bread from a basket.

"We seen squalls and tempests and sheets o' ice and hail the size o' turkey eggs smacking the deck like cannon shot." He passed her a plate heaped with what looked remarkably like leek pie. "Cap'n's got us through them all."

"How exciting!"

"At the time they were rather more unnerving than exciting," the captain said with a rueful smile.

"But to be a sea captain . . ." Callie sighed. "How did you come to be one?"

His gaze flickered to Patricia, then away.

"Quite by accident, Miss Ramsay." He offered her a glass of wine.

She lifted it high. "Then I propose a toast to new friends met upon the road quite by accident."

Patricia drank. Then she drank more. She ate very little. Her twisted stomach would not allow it. But wine went down easily. Calanthia maintained a steady stream of questions for him—some intelligent, others silly—to which he responded with apparent pleasure.

"Captain," Patricia finally blurted out at a pause in the conversation, "what news of our carriage horse? Will he be fit to take to the road tomorrow?"

"I fear not, madam. Your coachman tells me the animal's injury is long-standing and requires several days of rest."

"Is there another team to be hired here?"

"Unfortunately not."

"Then we shall simply take the wagon to our destination, Tricky. Won't that be marvelous? Auntie, you may ride upon the seat, of course." Callie giggled. Clearly she had had too much wine. Or perhaps her twinkling eyes were due to the attentions of the handsome, famous naval captain sharing their dinner.

"Mr. Rum will ride to the next village and command replacement cattle for you at the posting house there."

"Oh, sir, he mustn't." Patricia frowned. "We will be in your debt."

"As I am in yours for dinner tonight. We will be even then."

He did not smile. His smiles, it seemed, were all for the lovely girl grinning on the other side of the table.

Patricia stood abruptly, clattering her chair. She would not allow Calanthia to lose her heart to him. She was responsible for her sister's happiness, and a man who could make promises to a lady then nine years later upon a rainy road treat her as though he had never seen her before did not deserve the affections of a warm, spirited girl like her sister.

"It is time we retire, I think, Calanthia."

"Retire? Why, Tricky, it is only nine o'clock!"

"The mattress is goose-down," Aunt Elsbeth said. "Quite suitable for lovers."

All three of them turned their heads to her.

The captain grinned in comfortable amusement. "Miss Haye, you must be weary after the day's adventure. May I escort you to your quarters?"

Her hazy gray eyes smiled. "Terribly weary, young man. But fetch me that Mr. Rum now to see me up."

Calanthia tipped her glass to her lips. "Perhaps they will discuss Jacob's ladder next, and after that King David's dancing."

"I regret that Mr. Rum has already turned in for the night. A sailor's hours often follow the sun. Allow me, instead."

She batted his hand away. "No, no. I will see to myself." She wobbled toward the door, filmy shawl tailing upon the floor.

Patricia went after her, but she could not leave her young sister alone with a gentleman.

Calanthia leapt up. "I will go. She requires my assistance preparing for bed. But I shall return momentarily." She grinned up at the captain. "Don't drink all the wine without me." She followed Aunt Elsbeth from the room.

Silence descended, only the muted crackling of fire in the grate within, and the sounds from the taproom without.

"My sister, it seems, has lost all sense of propriety." She turned to him. "And she has drunk too much." She was not alone in that, and it was to no good cause. In the firelight, enhanced by candles, he was quite as breathtaking as he had been in the sunlight nine years earlier. The break in his nose lent his long, handsome face a dangerous air and his eyes glimmered with gold.

"Wine will not harm her." He tipped the decanter to the lip of his glass, then Patricia's.

"Thank you for your assistance today. Without it we might still be stranded upon the road."

"In which direction does your journey take you, Lady Morgan? Rum must inform the ostler at the posting house tomorrow morning." He offered her the glass.

She shook her head. No more wine. No more muddling her already muddled thoughts.

"Not much farther. Northwest."

He took a long swallow of his wine, set it down, and said, "Who are John and Ramsay?" His tone was easy. "It is the height of impropriety for me to inquire, no doubt, but I have spent a great deal of time removed from polite society, in fact years, so you must forgive me."

"They are my sons."

"I see." He went to the mantel, studying the painting hanging above it. "I imagined them perhaps your sister's suitors, but that was foolish of me. She would not speak of them so casually if it were so."

"She is familiar enough in her usual address that one might conclude such a thing."

"She is merely spirited. It suits her beauty." He spoke as though to the painting. "Yet she is not as lovely as her sister was at that same age."

Her heart beat so hard she feared he could hear it across the chamber. "I thought you meant to pretend we had not met before."

He turned to her, one corner of his mouth lifted in a slight smile.

"Why would I pretend that?" He spoke with perfect calm. Unregretful.

"Then," she managed beneath his untroubled regard, "perhaps you did not wish to expose me to my family's curiosity. I appreciate your discretion."

He walked to her until he stood very close. Too close for a lady and a gentleman who did not know one another.

"No particular discretion intended upon that account, my lady," he said in a low voice. "Only lack of opportunity to renew our acquaintance suitably. But I think it high time we finally introduced ourselves, don't you? And now you have no maidenly modesty to justify denying me the pleasure of your name."

His hand stole around hers, warm and strong and holding her with perfect confidence.

"Allow me to begin." He lifted her fingers to his lips. "I am Nikolas Acton." He placed the softest kiss upon her knuckles, his gaze fixed not on her hand or eyes, but her mouth. "And I am, as ever, enchanted."

CHAPTER FIVE

Patricia feared her hand trembled. *All* of her. He was large and broad-shouldered and warmth seemed to reach from his body to hers. And he smelled incredibly good—of wine and sandalwood and faint remnants of leather that made her want to close her eyes and simply breathe him in.

But her sister might return at any moment.

She tugged on her hand. "Captain, I must—"

"You must tell me your name," he murmured above her brow. "I have been waiting nine years for the honor, sweet Isolde, and have, I shall admit, grown somewhat impatient."

She melted. If the door had not opened she might have melted right into him.

He released her and moved away without hurry. Calanthia came across the room and took up her wineglass.

"Auntie informs me that if the mud inhibits our travels tomorrow, we shall find entertainment from a troupe of nearby players."

He chuckled. "Your aunt is charming."

"And I think *you* are charming, Captain. Oh! I hope I may say that." She flicked a questioning glance at Patricia. "Ladies enjoy flattery, but I do not know if gentlemen do."

"I should think that a gentleman who did not like pretty words from a pretty girl would be a great fool."

Calanthia glowed. Patricia looked between their pleased faces and a sick sensation lodged in her chest, tinged with panic.

"Ladies, I must bid you good night," he said.

"So soon?" Calanthia's lashes actually fluttered.

"Alas, yes." He bowed. "Miss Ramsay." He turned to Patricia and, with his back to her sister, lifted another languid half-smile, a glimmer in his rich eyes. "My lady, I look forward to renewing our acquaintance further tomorrow." He went out.

Calanthia threw herself into a chair.

"Oh, Tricky, isn't he marvelous? Why, we have known him less than a day and already it seems we have known him an age!" She played with the ribbons at her waist. "Do you think some individuals simply seem familiar to everyone due to a unique quality of character, or is it rather a special sympathy between one person and another that facilitates such pleasure in one another's company?"

Nine years ago she would have insisted the latter.

"What I think is that you have had too much wine tonight."

Her sister cast her an exasperated look. "I know Oliver made you believe that all men are cold fish, and I am sorry for it. But have you entirely lost the ability to appreciate a pleasing gentleman? I daresay, if Captain Acton does not meet us at breakfast tomorrow a thoroughly changed character, I may find myself with a raging tendre for him before the morning is out. He is positively *ideal*."

Ideal with Calanthia. And once, for an entire day, ideal

with her. And quite possibly ideal with every other lady who fluttered her lashes at him. Maidens and matrons alike. Matrons like *her*.

"Callie." Her throat felt inordinately tight. "Did you or Aunt Elsbeth mention to him or Mr. Rum that I am a widow?"

"I don't believe so. Auntie was mostly concerned with proving Mr. Rum wrong regarding the number of albatrosses aboard the Ark, and I never speak of your business, of course." She wrinkled up her nose. "According to the dowager, ladies do not gossip."

"Well, it would have hardly been gossip. It is not a state secret." But her palms were damp. She had not mentioned it to him either. "I am not certain that all sailors are quite as honorable as you imagine. I hope you will take care in becoming overly familiar with gentlemen we do not know."

"By that you mean Captain Acton, of course." Calanthia stood. "Well, all right, if you insist. But he helped us today when he needn't have, and I think he is perfectly amiable and you are unfair to him." With a sigh and a sleepy smile, she kissed Patricia upon the cheek, said "Good night," and went from the chamber.

Patricia stared through the open door, the noises of men drinking in the taproom quieter now. He had flirted with Callie, openly though mildly. He had flirted with herself as well, but with a clear suggestion in his eyes and words. Yet, apparently, he thought her married.

It hurt. She was surprised, and she felt like a fool for being surprised. She had, after all, long suspected he was not what he seemed.

She had noticed him first noticing her. Rather, staring at

her.

Seventeen years old, at the dull house party of distant cousins, she had welcomed the excitement of the May Day festival in a nearby village. Her male cousins were all enamored of sport and could not be counted on for diverting conversation. Her mother and the other ladies did nothing but sigh over the entertainments they were missing in London, which Patricia thought perfectly disingenuous.

"You do not even like London, Mama."

"Yes, but one needn't admit that publicly. Now button your pelisse and have a stroll about the garden if you have the fidgets."

But Patricia did not have the fidgets. Not the sort that could be thrown off with a stroll. It was much more than that, a humming in her blood that pressed at her to wake up and finally experience *life*. Perhaps London might answer that humming, but she was not to have her season until the following year.

A country May Day festival must suffice for the present.

So she donned her prettiest gown, tied her hair with pale pink ribbons, and danced about the May pole in the sunshine with her cousins and the farmers' and tradesmen's maiden daughters. She laughed and sang, and afterward, during a performance by a group of traveling players of the medieval love story of Tristan and Isolde, she saw him watching her from the other side of the crowd.

She ignored him. A lady, even one bursting from the seams of her life, did not encourage strange young men with stolen glances. Not even handsome young men.

Then she dropped her reticule—entirely by accident—and bent to retrieve it, and he was there, kneeling in the dirt, a smile on his lips and in his dark eyes.

"I believe this is yours, fair queen." He proffered her the reticule.

"You mean Queen of the Fair, I imagine." She knew her cheek dimpled by the way his gaze lingered upon it. "But if so, you have mistaken it, sir. It was not I who was crowned queen today."

"Then the judges were bribed to favor another. For you outshine any here." He unbent and she was obliged to look up. He was quite tall, dressed with casual ease and little fashion. His neckcloth was tied only in a knot, the buttons on his dark coat were tarnished, and his boots were decidedly scuffed as well as his trousers from kneeling. But Patricia barely noticed these insignificant details beneath the brilliant richness of his green eyes. Shadowed by a lock of nearly black hair, they reflected the laughter on his mouth. Whiskers dusted his chin and taut jaw, enough of a shadow to suggest a roguish carelessness about propriety. To her eyes so thoroughly weary of her family's variety of clean-shaven, stalwart manhood, he looked like heaven.

A smile tugged at her lips. "Thank you for retrieving my reticule." Fighting every instinct in her famished soul, she stepped away.

"But I have reconsidered," he said just over her shoulder.

She tilted her head aside as she continued through the crowd. Tables were laden with the produce of early summer, wildflowers, cheeses, berries, and baskets of raw wool. The music of pipe and fiddle wended its way through brays of donkeys, bleats of goats, and cheers over a fire swallower's daring.

"You have reconsidered?" She lifted a brow. "The judges were honest after all?"

"Absolutely not," he replied right behind her. "Charlatans, the lot of them."

She could not resist the lure of his playful tone. She paused at a stand of candied breads and tartlets crusted with berry jams that had bubbled through. She traced her fingertip along the edge of the table, delaying the inevitable. She should not speak with him. She should leave. She was the daughter of a peer. Peers' daughters did not consort with ramshackle young men at public festivals, no matter how charming they seemed. Her mother would have a fit.

"Then what have you reconsidered, sir?"

"That you are best served not having won the crown."

"Whyever not?" She flickered her gaze up. He stood close and her breath caught at the intensity of his rich eyes.

"The queen of the fair each year takes her victory march riding in the back of a wagon." His brow drew down in mock seriousness. "A wagon is not a suitable conveyance for a lady."

"What might be suitable?"

"Clouds," he said without hesitation. "Lined with silver, as when the sun shines through from behind." He scooped two tarts into his palm. He wore no gloves and his hands looked strong, sinewed and capable.

"Them's two pennies," the woman behind the counter grumbled.

"I haven't got it," he replied with a winning grin. "But I shall regret nothing greater, for I suspect, madam, that this tart could transform my humdrum existence into a sheer symphony of pleasure."

Twin spots of red popped out on the baker's round cheeks. She rolled her eyes and waved his hand away along with the pastries.

He bowed. "My humble thanks." He passed one tart to Patricia and the other to a tiny, hollow-cheeked boy poking his nose above the edge of the table, eyes wide. The lad grabbed up the treat and ran away.

He turned back to her. "Or the wings of a swan."

She smiled and nibbled the pastry, bemused, giddy, confused. Was this how gentlemen flirted, so cavalierly? She must go. She must not encourage him.

"What about swan's wings?" she heard herself say.

"An alternate suitable conveyance for a queen such as you." He reached for another tart. The baker smacked at his hand. He laughed and moved off, gesturing for Patricia to go before him. His fingertips grazed her elbow, holding for a moment then releasing her, and she had never felt such a slight touch so thoroughly. All the way to her toes.

"You are being ridiculous, sir." She feared she sounded breathless. She could not cease staring at him, his strong cheeks and jaw, and . . . She knew she ought not to have even noticed his firm, masculine lips. It was the epitome of ill breeding. She must leave.

"Am I being ridiculous?" They had come to the edge of a crowd. He paused and his eyes changed. Laughter still colored them, but something else as well. Something that made her insides trembly. "Rather—I fear—I am being smitten."

She wished to laugh but managed only a wavering smile. "You *fear* being smitten?"

He placed his hand across his heart. "Smiting is done with a weapon, madam. It is a foolish fellow who does not quake at sight of a blade, however lovely it appears."

A wild fluttering beset her breast. "You are likening me to a sword?"

"Possibly." His brow lowered. "Are you capable of wounding a man?"

"I should hope not!"

His expression lightened. "Excellent. Then I have nothing to fear, it seems."

She laughed. He bent his head, a lock of thick hair falling across his brow, and cast her the most perfect smile she had ever seen, at once conspiratorial and gentle. Her belly felt strangely warm. Everything in her felt warm. *Alive*.

She dragged her gaze away. They walked along the edge of the fair grounds where the animals to be judged were held between competitions.

"Aha. Here is the way life should be lived." He gestured to a pen of sheep.

"Whatever can you mean?"

"That these fellows know precisely where their next meal is coming from, and they spend their days simply enjoying the satisfaction of it."

She chuckled. "You are absurd."

"And you are smiling, which suggests that you are either as absurd as I, or too gracious to allow me to believe otherwise."

She could not hide her grin.

"Now," he said, stepping closer, "if you will favor me with the name of the lovely lady from whom I have nothing to fear, I shall account this quite the best day of my life and be as happy as these sheep. More so, I suspect."

"Oh, no, sir." She backed away, schooling her mouth into a line with difficulty. "We have not been properly introduced.

And indeed there is no one here who could perform the task." She nodded toward the contented sheep.

His brow furrowed as though he were pained. "But I must call you by some name." Abruptly, he brightened. "Choose a name—any name—and whatever it is—Helga, Broomhilde, Vladimir—it shall be all the more resplendent because it is bestowed upon you."

"*Any* name? I hardly know where to begin."

"Aha. But I do." He moved to her and this time she did not retreat. That something in his eyes that made her warm inside trapped her feet in one spot as he touched a single fingertip beneath her chin to lift her face. "I shall call you Isolde, and I shall be your Tristan. Theirs was a happy story, after all."

"Not the ending. And not at all for the king to whom she was wed," she said with a wry twist of her lips. Her heartbeat hammered.

He released her and seemed to consider this seriously. He glanced up, his emerald eyes sparking.

"Then, are you wed?"

She laughed. "No!"

"Betrothed?" And here his look seemed to suggest that he was not merely jesting.

She shook her head. "Not remotely. I have not yet enjoyed my first season in society."

He swept his hand before him. "Then we shall forget the royal husband entirely."

"But what of the tragic ending?"

"I propose we simply cut it off before it reaches the end."

"That sounds splendid." She nodded, laughter bubbling up. "Economical and optimistic."

"Indeed, propitious."

"Although perhaps a bit arrogant. I am not certain the medieval author of the story would like us altering it so blithely."

He waved that away as well. "Arrogance in the service of a happy ending must be tolerated. And, of course, Tristan was a knight. Arrogance was in his blood."

She cast him a glance as they walked along the fence. Her cousins would look for her. Or perhaps not. They were a large party and the festival extended a great distance from the village. Her absence might not even be noted until the end of the day when they gathered at the carriages to drive back to the house.

She peeked around the brim of her bonnet, drawn to look at him. Each time she did, she felt more as though she had known him before, as though his handsome face had always been part of her landscape of intermingled dreams and reality. And each time he returned her glance, her heart pounded faster.

"Then are you a knight, sir?"

"Nothing of the sort. I am the youngest son of a country squire, nearly finished university, with no land, no income, no profession, and generally no prospects to speak of." He came to a halt and smiled, but that odd light glittered in his eyes again. "Look at us, you without a London season yet, and I without a direction. We are both of us novices at life, it seems."

"It does seem so." She could not look him directly in the eye, but neither could she school her tongue. "I suppose we could learn something of life together." The words tasted dangerous and sweet. Rash, foolish, unladylike, and *divine*. "Now," she added.

He swallowed thickly, his loose neckcloth making the

action perfectly visible to her. Something about it caught at her belly.

He took the step that brought them together, grasped her hand, and held it lightly in his.

"I should not take this liberty, and I beg your forgiveness for it," he said in a low, strangely hoarse voice. His hand was large, his fingers warm around hers. It made her feel like sighing. Like singing.

"Then why have you taken it?"

"Because," he said quietly, "I wish to touch you."

"Like this?" Bold as she had never known herself, she slipped her fingertips through his and brought them palm-to-palm. She heard his heavy inhale and it moved her inside as though he drew breath from her. It was not real. Nothing about this was real. But it was the most real thing she had ever felt.

When, after a moment, he allowed her fingers to slip from his, she felt it like a loss.

"What will you do with yourself," she said in a desperate attempt to turn her thoughts from wishing for more of his touch, "now that you are an educated man of the world?"

He shrugged. "I haven't an idea."

"Well, what are you good at doing? Or what do you especially enjoy?"

He paused before a sheep pen fenced with sturdy wood and ran his hand along the top rung.

"My father and brothers would have it that I am good for doing nothing." He glanced up, his smile deep at one side, eyes alight. "And do you know, I quite enjoy obliging them in that."

She perked her brows up. "If I were a man, I would not hesitate to find the profession I liked best and at which I excelled."

"Wouldn't you?"

"I would!"

He crossed his arms, his roguish half-smile and the dark coat pulling at his shoulders sending the most curious, delicious eddies of heat through her stomach again.

"I think we should fix upon a profession for you," she said a little unsteadily. "Shall we?"

"If you like," he said, but his smile faded. She wanted it back again. She wanted that warmth in her belly to last forever.

"Hm. Where to begin?" She glanced at the pen behind him and donned a serious face. "Can you herd sheep?"

He twisted his lips ruefully and shook his head. Not the half-grin, but better than before.

"Of course not." She wrinkled her nose. "You are clearly a gentleman, so your pursuit must be gentlemanly."

He nodded in thoughtful agreement.

"Have you considered the law?"

"Absolutely not." He shuddered. "Far too contentious and tedious at once."

"The church?"

His brows shot straight up. He pointed a forefinger to his chest, and shook his head.

"I see," she laughed. "Then perhaps you could become a clerk of some sort. Do you know how to do sums?"

"I know that one and one together are two." His eyes sparkled beneath the afternoon sun.

Warmth crept into her cheeks. "Will you please attempt at least a modicum of sobriety?"

"It is very difficult when confronted with beauty that inebriates."

She pursed her lips. His gaze went straight to them and he said huskily, "In fact, I have never felt less sober in my life."

"My father drinks quite a lot." She spoke to control the spirals of nerves inside her. "He is a rather dull man and I believe it makes him feel alive. My brother, an affable fellow, fortunately prefers sport to rouse his spirits."

"And what, sweet Isolde, makes you feel alive?"

She could not hide her feelings. "Today," she whispered. "This."

And for a moment following those rash words—words truer than any she had ever spoken—pure, perfect longing stretched between them. He parted his lips to speak. Frightened at her own impetuosity, she did not allow it.

"I think your father and brothers are wrong," she said. "We must fix upon a profession for you so that you can make your name in the world."

He leaned back against the fence and spread his palms upward.

"I am as clay in your hands, fair Isolde. Fashion me as you will."

"But what can you *do*? You must tell me so that I will not be obliged to continue guessing."

His brow creased in thought. "Well, I can read, of course." His eyes glimmered. "I can ride. I can wield a sword and pistol. I can sail fairly well." He paused. "And I can, apparently, fall in love with a lady whose name I do not know within the course of a few short hours."

Her heart tumbled.

"You can . . . sail?"

"Fairly well," he murmured.

"Then you must join the Navy and become a great ship captain! You will be the scourge of Napoleon's fleet."

"Your confidence warms me, madam, especially as you are accepting my sailing ability wholly upon faith."

"But is that not what this day is about?" She spoke softly. "Faith?"

His eyes were very intense. "And hope."

And love. It was before them and between them, more powerful than anything either of them had known. But it could not be real. This was not reality. This was a dream. Ladies and gentlemen did not meet at country fairs and fall in love so swiftly. Did they?

She did not know. She only knew what her mother had taught her about men and women together, and it was not this—this longing to be near him, this sharp familiarity alongside the sheer newness of a man wholly foreign in every way she understood men to be.

"I wish to . . ." His voice trailed off. She waited, breaths short. His eyes shone wondering, like her heart. "I wish to give you a gift."

She smiled. "Is today not gift enough?"

"For me, yes. But a lady deserves something more. A posy, at the very least. Alas, I've a mere penny amongst the lint in my pocket. It will suffice for only a single flower."

"I will treasure it more because you have given it out of your want rather than your plenty."

He bought her a flower and she tucked it in her hair.

"You have spent your last coin. What will you do for dinner now?"

"I shall live upon the pleasure of this day and be well satisfied," he said quietly.

The sun dipped over the festival, spreading its ochre rays upon farmers and gentry. The music of pipe and fiddle, mandolin and drum accompanied them when the voices faded as they wandered side by side through fields of wildflowers flanking the fair grounds. Arms brushing, occasionally hands so that she quivered with feeling, they spoke of her anticipation to visit London the following year. He told her of the sights she would see—the great River Thames and the docks teeming with activity, the gothic splendor of Westminster Abbey, the figures at Madame Tussauds Wax Museum. He teased her about her lifelong rustication in the country and preened his town bronze to draw her laughter, and she did laugh and could not look away from his smile.

But as the sun's golden glow turned to red, their quips became fewer, their voices increasingly uneven, unable to support the levity of mere flirtation. The day would end, whether they would allow it or not, and so would their idyll.

They had not spoken in many minutes when he turned to her, grasped her hands and spoke quite unevenly.

"I fear, my sweet Isolde, that I have lost my heart to you." His vibrant gaze sought hers. "But how is it with you? Can you learn to love a man with no fortune, no prospects, nothing at all to speak of? A man who no longer even possesses his own heart?"

Her cheeks were flushed with heat, but she knew her eyes must sparkle for she saw the same bright hope in his.

"I believe I can. But I am not certain whether that man speaks to me now in jest or with sincerity."

"I have never spoken words more sincere."

"How can I know that?"

"Tell me your direction and I will call upon you tomorrow."

"Oh, I cannot. Papa and Mama would wish to know how we came to be acquainted and I would be obliged to tell them, and they will certainly like you less for it. But I cannot lie to my parents."

"Then I will leave it in your hands to decide, as a gentleman must." He looked quite like it was the most difficult thing he had ever said.

"But I do not know how it can be done!"

"Meet me tomorrow morning at the Maypole at ten o'clock," he said swiftly. "Bring a chaperone. Your maid. Your mother. Your entire family! Meet me tomorrow, sweet Isolde," he leaned in close to her, "and allow me to make your acquaintance properly so that I may then court you properly."

She trembled all over. "You will truly court me?"

"But not for too long, if you do not mind it."

She snatched her hands away. "Whatever can you mean, sir?"

He caught them again and pressed them to his chest. "That I do not wish to delay. For today fate has been infinitely generous to finally show me my life's course."

"And what is it?"

"To make you happy for the remainder of your days." He drew her close. "I vow to do so, my Isolde, if only you will consent to give me your heart."

"It seems improbable. Impossible. But . . ."

"But?" His voice was very low.

She whispered, "I think you know."

His chest rose in rough breaths. She could feel them upon her brow, then her cheeks as he bent his head ever so slowly and she, unsure, lifted hers. There was the warmth and scent of skin, the heady closeness, the unreality of it. For a moment, all suspended, neither moved, not fully trusting in the perfection of mutual feeling, the bliss of need and possibility. Then they submitted to the desire to be touching.

She had never kissed a man. He made it the most natural thing in the world.

He touched his lips to hers, their breaths trembling together. His hands came around her face, surrounding her in strength. He tilted her chin up, and he kissed her again, this time more certain, the sensation of his mouth over hers sublime, unreal, *perfect*. She reached for his arms and felt him beneath his coat sleeves, the unyielding muscle of a man, and it made her wild inside. Upon a sigh, her lips parted.

"Oh, my," she whispered, swept into sweet sensation. His hands tightened and he caught her mouth anew, and she wanted to move hers against his so she did. It felt good. Better than good. Like heaven. She opened her lips. She could taste him! His skin and lips, the lightest rasp of whiskers on his jaw. He tasted delicious. It filled her head, her body, with such pleasure, she sighed again.

His hands sank into her hair, drawing her closer, and their bodies brushed. His mouth covered hers fully, asking for more from her. She happily gave it, letting him kiss her as he wished, feeling him with her mouth and hands and then, daringly, pressing her body against his.

She had been astoundingly naïve. She felt him with *everything* and it was beyond pleasure. Beyond dreaming and reality entwined. She awoke completely, vibrantly alive, filled with feelings she had never before dared imagine. She could hardly bear such pleasure.

His hand swept down her back and he held her to him, and the tip of his tongue slipped along her lips, urging. She opened willingly, her hands sliding up his arms to his shoulders then into his hair. With her mouth she gave him what she was beginning to understand, but she wanted to be even closer.

She could not. She should not be doing this at all.

She broke away.

"I-I must go. It is late. I am expected at . . ." She could not finish. He stood perfectly still as she backed away, but his handsome face wore an expression as staggered as her own.

"Of course. You must go." His voice was rough.

"Perhaps I could stay for a moment longer," she said, returning a half step.

His chest rose and fell in heavy breaths. "All right."

"Just a moment." She inched forward again. "For I simply must go. Don't you see, the sun is nearly set?"

"I see one thing only."

She planted herself upon his lips, upon his chest, upon his everything. She wrapped her arms about his neck, he surrounded her with his embrace, and their kiss consumed. She wanted him to kiss her more, deeper, harder, and he did, and it was perfect, but it did not suffice. Inside she yearned so profoundly, a sort of ache his kisses filled yet also spread.

His hand curved around her behind and she gasped. But it felt right, and she wanted him to hold her like this, impossibly intimate, her hips pressed tightly to his. Then his tongue caressed hers and a strange and perfect shudder slipped through her. Around them the sounds of night were coming on, the singing of crickets and crackle of torches and lamps being lit. They had not been found in the daylight; they would be hidden in the dark if she remained. But she must return to the carriages before her family departed.

"I must go. I *must*."

He kissed her throat then her neck, his open mouth sending new pleasures through her.

"Stay with me, sweet Isolde," he said, his voice thick. "Ten minutes longer, I beg you."

"The sun has set." She clung to his shoulders, the caress of his mouth a drunken pleasure. "It will be dark soon."

"Stay."

"I wish to. I *cannot*." She dragged herself away. "The Maypole at ten o'clock tomorrow. You will come?" Abruptly apart from him, she felt uncertain. It all seemed so unreal in the failing light, her tender lips and pounding heart.

"Would that I were then and there already." His gaze seemed thunderstruck. But she was so worried. If she released this moment, it might vanish forever.

"But will you come? Promise me you will come and I will believe that you are a man of your word."

He nodded solemnly. "Yes, I will come. I promise it."

Perhaps he had. Perhaps he had been there at ten o'clock when she was standing in a drawing room three miles away, her family and friends congratulating her upon a betrothal that she had not known about until moments before, Oliver beside her with satisfied pride on his face.

Perhaps he had waited at the Maypole a quarter hour. Half an hour. An hour. Perhaps he waited until just before she managed to arrive there, racing the gig she stole from the stable by bribing the groom with her pin money, frantically praying, vowing that if he were there she would run away with him that very day rather than be married to another.

But he was not. Despite his declarations the previous night, he had not waited an hour for her. Or perhaps he had not gone at all. Perhaps he had forgotten her as soon as she refused him her favors the evening before.

She would never know. She could ask him directly now, but she did not trust in any response he would give. The naïve girl had not fully understood what he had wanted from her that night, but the married woman eventually did. Now she knew he was not the man she had longed for and dreamt of for months, commencing her marriage with lies that twisted her inside out. A man who would seduce another man's wife was not that fantasy. Captain Nikolas Acton was someone else entirely, and she should have known.

Chapter Six

Nik pressed the currycomb to his horse's neck and smoothed it along the sleek brown coat. He did not mind the labor. He had not forgotten the day when he'd had to perform this task himself, and others much worse, because he could not afford the price of boot blacking let alone a servant to apply it. Now the stable hand was busy assisting Carr with the carriage horse's poultice, and Rum had not yet returned from the posting house with the fresh cattle. And Nik liked his horse, a new purchase in London, an easy tempered animal with a degree of intelligence.

Unlike its master.

He should not have teased her the night before. He had done it out of anger. He saw the spark of interest in her cornflower eyes and abused it to soothe his pricked vanity.

But it was not truly vanity that pained him. It never had been.

She was married, changed by the years, yet he still wanted to touch her. He had wanted to touch her—needed to—from the first moment he saw her. For that reason alone he had teased her. But she was still married, and he was still the fool.

Footsteps sounded on the floor planking and a bright head appeared above the stall's half-door.

"Good morning, Captain. Have you breakfasted?"

He rested his arm across his horse's back. "I have indeed, Miss Ramsay."

"The rain seems to have eased. I daresay we will reach our cousins' house today. Has Mr. Rum returned yet with the new horses?"

"We may expect him shortly."

"I have nothing to do until then. May I help you?"

He smiled. "I would be glad for the company, of course, but I am afraid you are not quite dressed for the occupation."

"Neither are you." She unlatched the door and entered. "What shall I do?"

"Have you brushed a horse's mane before?"

"Never! What fun." She extended her hand. "A tool, please, sir?"

He handed over a brush and she set to work.

"I like it that you do not treat me as an imbecilic female."

"It requires no particular intelligence to comb out a horse's mane, Miss Ramsay."

"That is not what I mean, of course. You are very civil to me. Most gentlemen are impatient."

"Cads, all of them."

She giggled. "I am quite serious, Captain. My sister is wary of you, and tells me I must take care. But she has been disappointed in marriage and imagines all gentlemen unworthy of me, I think."

Nik had to force himself to continue working the curry-comb across his horse's coat, his gut tight. This information should make no difference to him.

"When was your sister wed?"

"It was 1807, the year Tricky spent the spring with our cousins. It has been all those years since she last visited them, in fact."

He pressed the comb into the bay's flank, the rhythmic action forcing steadiness to his breaths and heartbeats. How many times at sea as a young sailor had he set scrub brush to deck and labored in body to bring command to his thoughts? Each time, in those early years, he had thought of his father and brothers and how they would not believe the indolent, carefree Nikolas could force discipline upon himself so successfully. And during those long hours of hard work, earning experience and respect amongst his fellow sailors and superiors, he had also thought of her. He had always thought of her.

"In what month?"

The girl stroked the horse's hair with the comb, petting its neck with her other hand. "May."

Betrothed?

Not remotely.

He drew a slow breath. "Did your parents arrange the match, then?"

"Oh, yes. Papa was still alive, and he and Mama were quite heavy handed with Tricky and Timothy—that is our brother. But Papa died and now Timothy only listens to Mama when it pleases him. He is quite improved since succeeding to the title, actually."

The *title?*

"Your brother is Lord . . . ?"

"Bramfield. He is a viscount."

Viscount?

"It is not a particularly old title or grand estate, and so far north we may as well be in Scotland. But we were always well enough, and my brother is quite a solid member of Parliament now, though of course he tends to vote as his friends do."

A *viscount*. She was the daughter of a man so exalted she ought to have been confined in a parlor until she was wed, not dancing about the Maypole at a country fair. Yet she had fallen into his life like an angel, and into his arms like a farm girl, with her sparkling eyes and ready laughter, and her eager kisses.

He passed the currycomb across his horse's withers, seeking steadiness and not finding it this time. He *must* know.

"Your sister's husband's title. He—"

"Baronet, and quite wealthy. Mama and Papa were in alt over the match."

"They no longer approve of it?"

"Well, Papa is gone, of course, and Mama is now only interested in her charities, which she does entirely because the other ladies do them, you know." She added in a whisper, "She does not care for common people."

"And yet your sister fashions wedding rings for poor brides?"

"Oh, well, once Tricky was married she did as she wished, and she wished to do that. She is very kind. And clever. Much kinder and cleverer than me and our brother." She dimpled with pride. "And she is a very good example for others. She told me once she witnessed a gentleman's kind act and it inspired her. She said the act seemed perfectly natural to him, as though he hadn't even thought before he did it, and she wished to someday be the same—unaware of her own kind acts."

"What kindness had the gentleman performed, I wonder?"

"He gave a piece of bread or some such thing to a starving little urchin at a country fair. Is it not absolutely diverting that she would recall such a thing, or have even noted it?" She smiled fondly. "My sister has a soft heart, and I think I still have a great deal to learn from her."

He paused and the big bay gelding turned its head to regard him with dark eyes.

"Her husband must consider himself a fortunate man."

"Oh, well he *was* quite proud. He admired her greatly."

Nik knew he should not continue to pry. It was beyond indiscreet. But this girl seemed unaware of that, happy to share her family's secrets.

"He no longer holds her in such high esteem?"

"I suppose he might, if a corpse could." She slapped a hand over her mouth. "Oh, good heavens, that was horridly spoken! My brother in law is certainly a corpse, and I didn't like it at all how he abandoned Tricky to go off to war. But I should not speak of my own family member in such a manner. What must you think of me now, Captain?"

He thought her the most carelessly wonderful girl in the world.

She was a widow.

A *widow*.

Abruptly there seemed to be a great deal more air in the stable to breathe.

"She wears no mourning. How long has it been?"

"Oh, years. Nearly four. He died in Spain and *I* nearly perished with relief." She twisted her lips. "I am excessively unforgiving, my mother says."

"You are a girl who feels deeply. Strong emotion in a lady, Miss Ramsay, cannot be ill judged when it is sincere."

"Do you think so?" She cocked her head. "Mama and the dowager say otherwise. And of course gentlemen mustn't allow themselves to be overcome by strong feelings. Why, I suppose upon the sea it would be terribly foolhardy to act from emotions rather than rational thought."

He returned to his horse's back and the animal's head dropped in contentment. The hard life upon the sea had not allowed him to stew in regrets or anger. It had suited him perfectly well. Then.

"Oh, Captain, what a tremendous life you have lived! But one hears frightful stories of the lives of sailors. Was it truly horrid before you became your own master?"

"Challenging, both before and after. Being led by another man is not pleasant. But leading other men is a heavy responsibility." It all paled in comparison to the war within him now.

Years ago he would have gone directly into the inn and told her everything. He would have taken his chances, just as he had that spring day beneath the brilliant sunshine. He would bring a period to the insanity that had driven him for years to finish what they had begun that day.

But war had altered him and he no longer made rash starts. Nine years ago she had gone from his embrace to a bridal bed with another man. Nik had barely known her. But in those few hours he had changed. Meeting her and falling in love with her had altered the course of his life so dramatically she had simply become part of the structure of his reality. He might never see her again after today. But he could no more forget her than he could forget the sun.

"Will you return to sea soon, Captain?"

"The first of April."

"What a pity. We ladies on land will regret it." She stepped back from the horse. "There. How did I do?"

He forced a smile. "Quite well. If you were a stable boy I would toss you a coin."

She grinned. "All this work has made me famished, and my sister and Aunt Elsbeth will have risen by now. Will you take a cup of tea with us?"

"I will follow you shortly." And see her.

"Once we have taken to the road, will you still follow us?"

Probably for the remainder of his life. "That depends upon where you are going."

"Tricky, it happens that I am horridly jealous of you." Calanthia sipped her tea. "Captain Acton admires you."

Patricia's head snapped up from studying Oliver's letter.

Calanthia nodded. "Truly. He asked me all about your wedding, and Oliver."

Her stomach somersaulted. "He did?"

"Yes. It was wretchedly disconcerting, as I had gone to the stable to enjoy a pleasant flirtation with him and instead we spoke of you." She leapt up and swept her arms about Patricia's shoulders and pressed their cheeks together. "But I shan't hate you for it. If I cannot have him, I would not want anybody else in the world to have him but you."

Her throat beneath Callie's arm felt thick. "Must you be so vulgar, dear?"

"I thought I said it quite nicely! And it is *very* generous of me, really. I could eat him with a spoon."

Patricia tried to frown. She could not. He had asked about her wedding?

"I cannot imagine where you learn such language," she muttered instead, tucking Oliver's letter in her pocket to hide her quivering fingers.

"From Maggie."

"Your maid? Good heavens, I shall be obliged to turn her off."

"You cannot. She wears a ring you gave her, she is wed to our footman, and she believes she owes her happiness to you, which in fact she does."

Patricia moved toward the parlor door. She had not finished breakfast, but she could not eat now with her insides in a chaos. Why would he wish to know about Oliver? So he could determine whether Oliver would be the pistols-at-dawn sort of husband with his wife's lover?

Her cheeks burned. But since he had touched her the night before, she could not cease thinking of it. Might she live her fantasy upon this journey with *him*? She had not stipulated to herself that she must have a man of good character for her single night, only a man who could give her pleasure.

"Tricky, I told him Oliver died." Calanthia rushed the next words. "I know you do not wish strange gentlemen to know your particular business, but he is really quite lovely and anyway he sails again by month's end, so he shan't tell anyone."

"Month's end?"

The rumble of carriage wheels sounded in the yard.

"Oh. Perhaps that is ours." Calanthia sounded disappointed.

Panic welled in Patricia, but this time in the direct center of her chest.

They went into the foyer as Captain Acton entered the inn. He met her regard, and as though nine years had not passed and they still stood palm-to-palm beside a field of sheep, his eyes seemed to seek something within her. She had the most unwise urge to blurt out that he might still find it there.

"Your carriage is readied," he only said. "Your horses will remain here as long as you wish. I have given instructions to the stable master that if any particular care is required for the injured animal I will return within two days and see to it." No trace appeared of the teasing rogue from the night before, only gentlemanly concern.

"Thank you. You are very kind."

He bowed.

"Oh, no," Calanthia exclaimed. "Then we must part now, Captain. Are you near your destination?"

"I am, but I shall suffer for loss of such charming company." He looked at Patricia again. "Shall I have the team walked or are you prepared to depart?"

Could he have come back into her life now only to leave it again so swiftly? Even if he were the sort of man who would try to seduce a married woman, she did not want him to go yet. But abruptly it seemed he would.

She must make him wish to remain.

"We are prepared. Calanthia, will you inform Aunt Elsbeth?"

Her sister cast a regretful look at the captain and disappeared up the stairs.

His smile faded.

"You are a widow."

She had not expected this. But he had never been what she expected.

"I am."

He stepped closer. The foyer abruptly seemed quite small. He wore an elegant greatcoat and held a fine hat in his hand, and he was the most perfect man she had ever seen. He had always been, even in tarnished buttons and smudged boots.

"You wear a betrothal ring." His voice was low.

"It is not the ring my husband gave me. That is a family heirloom and is now in the vault for John's bride someday."

"Your son is quite young. You might still wear it."

"I would rather wear this." Her breaths felt tight. "I made it for a girl who perished the day before she was to be wed. Her groom could not bear for it to become another's ring, but he could not bear to keep it either."

He grasped her hand, lifted it between them, and the pad of his thumb passed over the diamond chips set in gold. He must be able to feel her tremors.

"Does it deter gentlemen? As it did me?"

"You did not seem deterred last night. But perhaps you only intended to tease."

His eyes glimmered. "Perhaps."

"And I . . ." She gathered her courage. "I was not entirely unhappy about it."

A crease appeared in his brow, but he did not speak.

"Say something," she whispered.

"Why didn't you tell me yesterday that you are not married?" His voice sounded gravelly.

Her eyes went wide. "The occasion for it did not arise."

"You might have."

"I might have, yes. When you appeared on the road I could have said, 'Good day, sir. Although we have not met in nine years I would have you know now, before you assist us with our carriage, that I am a widow.'" She lifted her brows. "Would that have sufficed?"

He seemed to breathe in deeply, and the corner of his mouth tilted up.

"Here again is the girl I met that day, quick-tongued and certain of her own mind." He scanned her features. "Yet more beautiful now than she was then."

She knew not where to look. Only he had ever spoken to her like this, and she had forgotten how it confused her. But she had not forgotten how it made her deliciously agitated inside.

"You needn't flatter me," she whispered. "I have already suggested to you that I am susceptible. As I was then."

"Susceptible to teasing and flattery?"

She lifted her gaze. "Susceptible to you."

He took another breath, a bit ragged it seemed. Then he gripped her hand and pulled her to the parlor. She stumbled after, he shut the door, and like that first day—that only day—his hands came around her face and he lowered his mouth to hers.

CHAPTER SEVEN

He had never forgotten the texture of her lips, the sweet humidity of her breath, the taste of her tongue or scent of her skin. In every woman he had touched since then he had searched for glimmers of her and found none. Now he took her mouth beneath his and fell into sunlight again.

As on that day so long ago, she met him eagerly. But in the intervening years she had spent as a married woman, one thing about her kiss had not changed. He drew away and looked into her upturned face, her cheeks aglow. She was so beautiful to him and he held her in his arms again as he had dreamt. But this could not be right.

He could not mask his incredulity. "You have not been kissed?"

"Wha—what?" Her hazy eyes were fixed upon his mouth, her breaths quick. She wanted to be kissed, but she possessed no skill at it whatsoever.

"Did your husband never kiss you?"

Her brows cut downward, the pleasure slipping from her face.

"Are you insulting me?"

"Observing. In astonishment."

She ducked out of his embrace and halfway across the chamber, pressing her palms to her cheeks.

"No, he did not kiss me. At least not—" Between her fingers her face flamed. "Not like you did."

He stared, and probably his mouth hung open. Alongside the incredible satisfaction that apparently she had only him with whom to compare her husband in this matter came a sort of sticky nausea.

"But you have two children."

She cast him a sharp look. "It does not require the attachment of mouths to conceive a child, Captain Acton."

For a moment he could not speak. This was too unbelievable to accept. He finally managed words.

"Was he *blind*?"

"Are you trying to be cruel or is it merely an unfortunate byproduct of your incivility?"

He moved toward her; he could not remain distant watching her eyes so fraught with distress. He reached for her and she flinched back but he curved his hand around her delicate jaw and into her hair. Her eyes were wide, lashes fanned about the blue, her nostrils flaring slightly and lips parted. Nik's breaths slowed through pure wonderment. How a man could gaze upon this and not wish to kiss every inch of it, he could not fathom.

"Was he disinterested in women?"

Her eyes shot wider yet. "No. He was quite fond of me in that manner." Her gaze shifted away. "Quite," she whispered.

Red washed across his vision. "Men can behave as beasts."

She ducked her head again. "He was not a beast. He did not

beat me or employ force. He was only . . . cold." She was breathing heavily. "I cannot believe I am speaking to *you* of this."

He threaded his fingers through her hair and touched his lips to her brow. God, how he wanted to feel her in his hands and upon his lips forever.

"Not all men are cold. You inspire quite the opposite in one man in particular."

She remained perfectly still in his hold. "Despite my lack of experience with kissing?"

Where silken skin met satin hair, he drew in her scent of honeysuckle and woman. "That can easily be amended."

"I hoped you would see it that way." She went onto her toes and pressed her lips to his.

What she lacked initially in skill she more than made up for in enthusiasm. Her mouth sought his and Nik forgot that she knew nothing about kissing in the sheer pleasure of teaching her how.

She was a quick learner, and she learned with her entire body. In response to his urging her lips parted, and he tasted her as he had dreamt of tasting her again for years. She was hot and wet within, her tongue supple and tentative, and he took her gently at first, then deeper, until they were locked in the kiss. His cupped her face then her shoulders in his palms, savoring the beauty of her slender shape. She spread her hands upon his chest, her fingertips pressing in as her hungry mouth opened to allow him entrance. He stroked her heat and damp beauty and she moaned lightly and brought her body against his.

He had been waiting years to touch her again. She responded so readily. And swiftly he wanted a great deal more than kissing. He drew away from her lips but his heart pounded and she must be able to feel his desire now.

Her lashes fluttered open to reveal cornflowers veiled in haze. Her lips, dark pink and tender from his kisses, parted upon a little sigh. "Did I do well?"

"Too well."

She licked her lips and he restrained the urge to drag her against his arousal. Instead he slid the tip of his tongue over her full bottom lip then took it between his teeth. She moaned, a soft sound of pure want, and opened entirely beneath him, and Nik found himself in a hired parlor preparing to strip a woman naked and lick every part of her before she could tell him nay. She slid her hands into his hair and accepted his mouth on the curve of her throat where her fragrance maddened him as it had before. Just as then, he knew he must halt this. Before he lost the will to halt.

But good Lord it was hard halting. And he was hard, and she wasn't making it any easier, pressing her sweet thighs to his and shifting sensuously like a cat seeking caresses. Her slender hands slid inside his coat, grasped the waistband of his breeches, and she rubbed against him, another moan slipping from her. He felt it in his mouth upon her throat and in his aching cock, and he pushed her back into the door and let himself feel her like she wanted to be felt. She obliged, spreading her knees, gripping him tighter and whimpering in surprised pleasure.

"Dear God." He grasped her arms and pressed his mouth to her cheek. "We must stop this," and recommence in a more private location, preferably without a carriage waiting to steal her away from him again, and preferably with his ring upon her finger. He wanted her, he had always wanted her, and she clearly wanted him too. Fate could not be so kind. But it seemed fate was offering him another chance with this woman, despite the shortcomings of character and position in the world with which he had been born, yet perhaps because he had worked so hard to remedy those.

"But— But I— I do not want to stop." Beneath his coat her hands slid up his back. She pressed her breasts to his chest, her belly to his, her entire intoxicating body, nuzzling his jaw. "And this time it is *my* carriage waiting and *my* life and I can do what *I* wish."

Amidst the crush of desire to help her do what she wished with alacrity, Nik had to smile. He drew back to look into eyes wide with defiant beauty.

"It is indeed." His throat was thick.

"Is it what you wish?" Her breaths came fast.

He brushed a silken autumn lock back from her brow, the sensation of her skin like a drug. "Most assuredly."

"Good, because I hoped you would assist me with something." Her throat constricted in a lumpy swallow. "I need a man at the present and I would like it to be you."

He froze. *At the present?*

"To assist you further upon your journey?"

"No. For another purpose. I would like a night of— of— of." Her lashes dipped. "A *night*."

"A night?" was all he could manage aloud.

"Only a night." She spoke quickly yet quite firmly. "I shan't expect more. Calanthia told me you are setting off to sea again shortly which suits me well since I only have need of a man for this one night. A single night and I shall be satisfied."

Abruptly it became difficult to draw breath. He released her and stepped back. He had, it seemed, been dreaming again. She was a titled lady and he may as well still be the penniless youth whose flattering attentions she had enjoyed and who she left waiting while she ran off to marry a baronet. A war hero might do for the Miss Chapels of society, but apparently not for Lady Morgan.

"A single night." His voice came forth unevenly. "Like that single day?"

"Well, yes. Although rather more involved, as it were."

"You cannot be serious." He could not bear it if she were.

"Of course I am. Don't you see? It was providence that brought you here."

"Providence."

"Yes, providence. And perhaps a degree of coincidence. You see, I know— I *knew* after I had been married some weeks and learned—" She broke off, momentarily flustered. But she regained her purpose swiftly. "I understood what you must have wanted from me that day. And I can see it in your eyes that you still do."

Nik's palms went cold. "What do I want from you now that I wanted then?"

"To . . . *be* with me."

Even as he wished to strip her beautiful body of clothing and *be* with her as soon as possible, nausea rose in him again.

"Is that what I wanted?"

Her brows snapped down. "Don't look at me that way. I am not perfectly naïve any longer. I am a widow and may speak of such things, if I wish, with a man who wants it as I do."

"You are not speaking of anything. You have not yet used

any words to the point." He controlled his tone with the greatest effort. If she were any other beautiful widow he met upon the road he might oblige her. But, no. Not now that he had found his Isolde again. No other woman now would do. But not like this, only for a moment as he'd had her before. "If you are not the naïve girl you were, then say the words so we have no misunderstanding between us now, as apparently we did then."

"I want you to . . ." Her voice fluttered.

"To?"

"I-I want . . ."

He moved to her again, grasped her upper arms and bent over her head.

"You want me to make love to you for a single night?"

Not looking him in the eye, she nodded. For a moment of silence he held her and told himself it was the last time. Dreams were for careless youths, not grown men. Not for him any longer.

"If you cannot say it, Lady Morgan," he finally uttered as the despair of years of wasted hope washed across him, "my guess is that you should not be doing it." He loosened his grip and she sagged against the door.

"Are you that sort of man, then?" Her voice seemed brittle. "The same as my husband? I never imagined it after the way you teased me that day, and last night. And the way you kiss me."

"The same as your husband?"

His voice was deliciously deep and menacing. He stood so close. Patricia longed to reach out and touch him again, to make him continue kissing her. But his jaw was hard now, his shoulders rigid.

"Trust me, Lady Morgan, when I take my bride to bed I will not leave her longing for kisses while I do my duty upon her."

She knew not why her cheeks should flush at his plain speaking. She only knew that this had gone horridly wrong.

For all that was holy, she did not understand men! All Oliver had ever wanted of her was her body to lie with. Now, despite every lesson she had ever learned in ladylike comportment, she was offering this man precisely that, and he seemed *angry*? But perhaps he imagined she was trying to inveigle him into a permanent arrangement. Everybody knew rogues avoided that sort of commitment. She must be perfectly clear.

"I do not want *duty* from you. Far from that. I want . . . pleasure." There, she had said it aloud, and it did not even matter that her cheeks were like lit coals and her body like someone had taken a warmed poker and slid it beneath her dress to touch her quite intimately. It felt spectacular, and she simply must make him understand. "For a night," she finished on a whisper.

The door rattled. She leapt away from it.

"Tricky!" Calanthia rushed in. "Aunt Elsbeth is missing!"

"Missing?"

"I have searched everywhere. She is not here." She twisted her hands together.

"Do not fret, Miss Ramsay." His voice was even now. "I will instruct the innkeeper to allow you to look into the private chambers and Mr. Rum, your coachman, and I shall search the public rooms and outbuildings. Your aunt will be found, never fear."

Calanthia's lower lip trembled. "Oh, thank you, Captain.

You are very good!"

He nodded, cast a thoroughly contrary glance at Patricia, and left the parlor. She took a deep breath and followed him.

Patricia and Calanthia searched the inn from kitchen to garret. In the foyer once again, Callie put her hands to her face.

"It is all my fault," she groaned. "I only left her alone for several minutes—ten perhaps—to speak with . . ." Her cheeks colored and her gaze darted away.

"To speak with whom?"

"A gentleman watering his horses without, if you must know. But it seems he was with a party of people, and the young lady called him by his given name, although she had an unattractively large nose. But I suppose very nice men don't care about that sort of thing. In any case, I came back inside and discovered Auntie's absence. I feel positively wretched!"

Patricia could not very well reprimand Callie for her flirtation in the yard when she herself had been engaged in a much more flagrant indiscretion in the parlor. Flagrant and delectable and heart stopping and *would her longing for him never cease?* No. She was destined to yearn hopelessly for him forever, it seemed.

"Well, nothing can be done for it now. We must find her."

"Thank you for not reprimanding me." Callie's voice was thoroughly subdued. Patricia drew her sister into an embrace and stroked her bright locks.

"You are full of admirable spirit, my dear, and I am not the dowager or even Mama to chastise you." Her hand stilled upon Calanthia's hair.

She was most decidedly not her mother or the dowager,

and she might feel all the feelings a woman could feel *at once*. She needn't cordon off pleasure and passion into one night. Why hadn't that occurred to her before? Perhaps because she had never before ached to kiss a man from sunrise to sunset to sunrise again?

"No doubt Aunt Elsbeth has only gone to a shop in the village. We will find her," she murmured, heartbeat speeding. He had not rejected her. He had kissed her with knee-weakening ardor and said he wanted her right up until she declared she only needed him for one night. Perhaps . . .

Perhaps she was the greatest idiot alive. She must have misunderstood him. Perhaps his teasing when he believed her still married stemmed not from roguishness, but . . . *What?* She did not know! She only knew that his kiss felt as honest and true as it had years ago, and as thoroughly passionate.

She gripped her sister's hands. "As Captain Acton said, do not fret."

She grabbed their cloaks off the hooks. Rain fell in a steady gray drizzle again as they crossed the yard to the street, half boots sinking into mud and hems soaking up puddles.

Aunt Elsbeth was not to be found in any shop. They turned their eyes to the church at the street's end.

"Perhaps she wished to consult with the vicar on that albatross question?" Callie suggested.

"That must be. You look there, and to be thorough I will circle around the green then meet you back at the inn." They parted and she picked her way between puddles to the commons flanking the village. In the rain the pasture was a sodden blanket of emerald and brown stretching a distance. She prayed Aunt Elsbeth had not wandered here, trying not to think about the creek that must pass somewhere nearby, or a well, or stile, or any other place in which an elderly lady might come to grief.

Mounds of white rose up in the mists and became sheep. Several turned their heads at her approach, at ease in the drizzle, quite as though it mattered little whether it rained or shone or tempests raged. They stood content in their pasture, life lived without pain, regret, doubt or unfulfilled longings like she had been living with for years. *Years.*

Sheep—stupid sheep—knew better than she how to live life, as a young gentleman had once playfully suggested.

But there had been wisdom in that jest. Not that she must stoically accept life as it rained upon her. No, she had done that for years. Instead she should embrace the life that lived naturally within her, life yearning for a man who made her laugh and thoroughly breathless at once.

She smiled, and felt weak all over, and knew quite suddenly that all along she had not wanted any man with whom to experience passion. She had wanted *him.* Over the years the man who brought her pleasure in every one of her fantasies had rich emerald eyes, a carefree smile, and hands whose touch turned her inside out. Now he was no longer a fantasy. He was real, he had a name, and he had kissed her far beyond her fantasies. Then he had denied her a single night. Because, perhaps, he wished for *more* than one?

He must not disappear again. The mere idea of it made her light-headed with panic.

She turned to follow the bend in the fence. He stood there, mere yards away on the other side. Rain dripped off his hat and onto his broad shoulders. Patricia's thumping heart hurt so powerfully she pressed her hand to her chest.

The corner of his mouth ticked up, reluctantly, as though he could not prevent it. He gestured toward the sheep. "We must stop meeting like this."

She released a taut breath. "I am sorry."

"For exactly what, I wonder?"

"Good heavens, what a perfectly dreadful rain!" Aunt Elsbeth stepped out of the mist. Bonnet flowers bobbing, she teetered toward Patricia. Captain Acton scaled the fence and took her arm.

"Miss Haye, we are happily met again. Tell us if you will, what have you seen upon your perambulations today?" He smiled down at the myopic old lady with genuine warmth.

Patricia found she could not move, but only stare. For five years married to one man she had felt nothing but toleration. Yet two days spent with this man over a decade and her heart it seemed had become entirely his.

She had mistaken his intentions the night before. She *must* have.

"Sheep, sheep, and more sheep." Aunt Elsbeth shook her head, splattering rain from her hat in all directions. "But it seemed the only way to bring you here."

"You wound me, madam. You needn't have lured me to this pasture on a false pretense. I would quite gladly follow you anywhere." His gaze shifted to Patricia for an instant, sharp and direct.

"Not me, you silly man." Aunt Elsbeth batted him on the sleeve. "My niece, of course. It is about time the two of you encountered one another amongst sheep again."

Patricia's heart tripped. "Good heavens, Aunt, what do you

mean?"

"I haven't any idea." She shook off the captain's escort and walked with tottering purpose toward the inn.

His brow creased.

"I never told a soul," Patricia choked out.

For a moment he regarded her silently. Then, "Of course you did not." Without another word, he went after her aunt.

CHAPTER EIGHT

She and Calanthia bathed Aunt Elsbeth, dressed her in woolens, ladled broth into her, and put her to bed. By the time they were free to change their own clothing, the light in the rainy sky was failing. Patricia donned her white muslin gown threaded with silver embroidery and pearls, and arranged her hair carefully with combs.

"This dress is inappropriate for this weather," she mumbled as Calanthia fastened her into it. But she felt like herself again, the girl she had been when she first met him, full of the excitement of life's mysterious offerings.

"You are beautiful," Calanthia said with unaccustomed quiet. "Almost mystical."

"Are you well, Callie?"

"If I had not been so foolish, Aunt Elsbeth would be joining us for dinner now, or we would already be at our cousins' house."

"Our cousins can wait," and whatever errand Oliver had set her upon. She would not be dictated to by her husband ever again. Or by anyone else. Beginning now she would follow her heart. "You are the best sister I could ever wish for. Merely young, but that is no crime, nor the feelings that drive you to do what you will now."

With a bit more spirit Calanthia went with her down to the parlor. The captain stood by the hearth, firelight dancing over the planes of his face.

"Ladies, you are resplendent." He smiled at Calanthia then turned to Patricia. "How does Miss Haye do this evening?" he only said, but his eyes, warm and focused so steadily upon her, said much more. They said that perhaps he had forgiven her. That perhaps he was no longer angry.

"She does well. You are still here," stumbled off her tongue.

The edge of his mouth lifted. "I am indeed."

"As am I, by the way," Calanthia quipped. "But I suddenly find myself enormously sleepy, and now rather wish to take my dinner in my chamber with Aunt Elsbeth." Her gaze darted between them. "If you will forgive my hasty departure, Captain? I hope we will see you in the morning before we depart."

He bowed again and before Patricia could argue, her sister was gone. Then they were alone and her knees went watery. She forced words.

"Thank you for your assistance again, with my aunt this time. One does not wonder that you are an acclaimed hero in the estimation of society."

His eyes sparkled. "And in your estimation, Lady Morgan?"

"A hero, most assuredly," she repeated his earlier words.

His look grew cautious. "Because I sink French vessels upon the ocean and rescue ladies stranded upon the road?"

"Because you once showed me that life needn't be lived according to what others expect, and although I was afraid to live it then, I have held onto that vision for nine years. And because you are here now when you might have left."

He drew a deep breath. Then another. He did not move, the space between them flickering with golden light.

"I think I have lost my appetite for dinner," he said.

Oh, God, *would he leave her now?*

"Have you?"

"But perhaps I am mistaking it." His voice was gorgeously husky. "The trouble is, I cannot seem to think at all with you standing there like an angel."

"Captain—" she whispered.

"Nik."

"Do not tease me."

"After eight years at sea I have no true teasing left, sweet Isolde. Only, I need you."

The breath went out of her. "You—?"

He crossed the chamber in three strides, tilting her face up with a strong hand, and spoke above her lips. "I need you and it is driving me mad. So unless you wish to be ravished presently upon the floor of this parlor, I recommend removing yourself to a chamber with a bed in it, with haste."

Wide-eyed, tongue tangled, she nodded and drew from his hold. He let her go. But as she reached the second story she heard his tread upon the stair and glanced back. Below in amber lamplight his eyes shone.

"Do not imagine I am allowing you out of my sight again," he whispered above the noise from the taproom. "Just see where that got me before."

She laughed aloud. He mounted the steps, grasped her hand, and dragged her through her bedchamber door then into his arms.

It required remarkably little time for him to divest her of gown and petticoat, then shoes and—with deliriously capable hands—stockings. During this blissfully divine activity she apologized.

"I have not done this in some years. You must forgive m—"

He caught her mouth beneath his as his fingers worked at the lacing up her back. She clutched his shoulders, arching against him, and pushed at his coat to rid him of it, then his waistcoat.

But she was not finished apologizing.

"I am sorry I did not tell you the truth immediately."

Her corset fell away and his hands swept beneath her breasts, cupping her through her shift with perfect command. She gasped and a sound of masculine pleasure rumbled deep in his chest. He kissed her lips, her throat.

"I-I am sorry I thought you were the sort of man who could be propositioned."

Their breaths came fast, only his thumb tracing a languid spiral around her nipple. She ached for him to touch it.

"Is this what you wanted when you asked me for a single night?" Slowly, so slowly now, he passed the pad of his thumb across the sensitive peak. Sweet agony rippled through her.

"Yes."

He picked her up and bore her to the bed, and dragged her hips beneath him. "This too?" He covered her breast with his palm and moved against her, parting her legs with his knees until she was flush against the ridge of his arousal. "Is this what you hoped I would give you?"

She made a sound like a groaning whimper. It was too good, feeling him. "God, yes. Yes."

He teased her nipple through the thin linen of her shift. She pressed into him and his hand came around her thigh. She struggled for air. He was *touching her*—her skin beneath his, touching his.

"Nik, I—"

"Is this what I would have taken from a gently bred maiden?" He stroked the tender inside of her thigh, his heat and touch all for her, bringing her body to life.

She reached for the fly of his trousers. "You did want this then, didn't you?"

He grabbed her hand and stilled her.

"I would not have been a man if I had not wanted to make love to you that day. But I would not have taken it if you had offered."

"Why not? Was I not—?"

"You were perfect." He traced the line of her lips with the tip of his tongue, stealing her breath. "Perfect."

She trembled, every part of her aching for him.

"Please do it now," she whispered. "It has been years, but I should be able to manage . . ." Her words petered out. A smile lurked about his lips. He pulled away and tugged off his boots then his shirt, and began on the fastenings of his trousers.

Air puffed out of her in little bursts.

"Will you blow out the candles now?" *Please God, no.* Oliver had never undressed before her, but even if he had there was no comparison. She drank in the vision of Nik's muscles, sleek and powerful, and the line of dark hair that drew her attention downward. He was pure breathtaking male, from the jagged scar crossing one shoulder all the way to—

She snapped her gaze away. *Good heavens.* The Americans

had gotten it quite wrong. All men were not created equal.

She sought for words, any words. "How on earth did my aunt know about your scar?"

"Soldier. Likely guess." He spoke roughly, quick. His eyes scanning her seemed molten, his gaze so intense.

"So, will you blow out the candles?" she repeated, voice quite small.

"No."

"But I thought—"

"I have dreamt of this for years. I will not be denied the sight of you." He caught her hands and held them to the counterpane, palm-to-palm, then covered her open mouth and came into her with his tongue in shallow, tantalizing strokes. She pressed against him, seeking the sensation of his arousal against hers. His hands moved her hips against his and her need spiraled.

She broke free of his kiss.

"Please, Nik. Please, now."

Swiftly he pushed her shift up and she wiggled to get beneath him fully. But he did not stop at her waist as she expected, tugging the linen over her breasts and sweeping it free of her arms and hair.

"Dear God. So beautiful." His hands, large and rough, circled her waist then slipped up and over her breasts.

"*Oh!*"

He covered her with his mouth. She had never imagined it, never fantasized this, never knew such a thing could be. He sucked on her breast, his mouth wet and hot, and stroked the peak with his tongue. *Too* good. Too unbelievably good. She whimpered and strained to him, damp heat throbbing at the crux of her legs. Then he touched her there, and she went wild. He caressed with his beautiful hand like he belonged there, like she belonged to him to do with as he wished. She rocked against him, unable to withhold her cries, all modesty cast off. He took her nipple harder and his caressing tongue made her frantic, the wicked play of his fingers seizing her below, so sweet and hot and unending. She died. She *was* his. He might touch her forever and she would live for this alone.

Gasping for breath, she collapsed into the mattress, pleasure curling through her.

Then came awareness again. And embarrassment.

"What happened?" She retracted her limbs from the man around whom she had wrapped them. "I— Why didn't you make love to me?"

He took up her hand and pressed his mouth to it, then flattened it against his chest, and laughter came beneath her palm.

"Remarkable as it seems to me," he said roughly, "I am still making love to you."

She stiffened. "I-I don't understand. Are you *bored*?"

He pulled her under him and she felt him entirely, his hips against her soft inner thighs and his hot, hard shaft where she throbbed.

"Rather, I am overly eager." With slow thrusts he caressed her and it was heaven, scandalous and sensuous. He did this to her, with her, making her want him more than she thought possible, and she moaned, feeling him with her body. Oh, God, she felt him *everywhere*. She threaded her fingers through his hair, thoroughly abandoned to the pleasure.

"But— W-what are you waiting for?" she managed to utter.

Flames leapt in his emerald eyes. "For you finally to tell me your name."

Her breaths failed.

"Patricia," she whispered. "My name is Patricia Ramsay."

"It is a pleasure to make your acquaintance, Patricia Ramsay."

She was his. Finally, after nine years, he took possession of the woman who had filled his dreams without ceasing. Muscles straining, Nik pressed forward then retreated, with each stroke delving deeper, and finally he entered heaven in a woman.

He could not control his shaking. He had thought he wanted her before. Now embedded in her he knew raw need so powerful it seized the air in his lungs. But he could not go on. She was beautiful, her exquisite breasts, her legs and her hot, wet womanhood dragging him in deeper.

But she was entirely immobile.

"Patricia." The word came out ragged.

Her eyes flickered then opened, two hazy pools of blue. Swiftly the blue turned bewildered.

"Nik?" Her voice quavered.

He swallowed hard, pressing his lips to her damp brow.

"You may move." Dear God, if circumstances did not alter swiftly he might end up finishing matters before they even got started. The sensation of her thighs about his hips and her belly beneath his had him paralyzed, all but the rush of blood to one place.

"I may?" she peeped.

"You may. In fact it is especially encouraged." Knowing he was probably making a grave mistake in terms of his diminishing self-control, he slipped his hand along her shoulder and over her breast, trailing his fingertips around the peak he'd had in his mouth minutes earlier. Her eyelids fluttered and her hips shifted. He sucked in a breath and moved against her. He caressed her nipple again, then stroked slowly and steadily into her. She moaned softly, her back arching, sinking him deeper. He struggled for command.

She stretched her head back and sighed. "Oh, Nik. This is sublime."

If she was still able to speak, it was not yet sublime enough for her. He trailed his tongue along her throat, kissed her sweet, swollen lips, and thrust to his length. She gasped. He pulled out and thrust again. This time she met him.

"*Ohh.*"

"Like that." *Dear God.* Again. "*Patricia.*" And again. He rode her and her hands grabbed at him, pulling him in hard. She was perfection, sweet and hot, her pliant body, her cries, his name upon her tongue.

"Nik, I want—" She took him in completely, her damp lips parted. She pressed her palms to his back. "I want this." He drove into her, meeting her core, caressed by her until he was mad to fill her. Yet still she took from him, fingertips digging into his muscle, forcing him to her over and over, making him pleasure her while he held on beyond insanity. She hooked her strong, slender leg about him and her heel dug into his backside, trapping him. If she desired, he would be trapped forever. But his need could no longer wait. He grabbed her hips and dragged her against him.

"*Never,*" she uttered. "Not like this," and with stuttered cries shuddered beneath him. He released deep. Hard, sudden and blinding. Just as he had fallen in love with her—hard, sudden, blinding.

He sucked in air, grappled for his mind, his sanity, his very person. But they were not to be found. He had lost them. Again. To her. This time eternally.

He pushed onto his elbows and her grasp on him loosened. He stroked damp-darkened tendrils of hair from her brow. Her eyes closed, lips curving into an infinitely sweet smile, and silently they shaped the words *thank you*.

A grin tugged at his mouth, but for what did she thank him? Her single night of pleasure?

"Rather, thank you," he murmured, kissed her tempting lips, and pulled himself off her. She curled up on her side, tugging the coverlet to her chin, her smile lingering.

He could not be so sanguine. Brow pressed to the counterpane, he tried to slow his pulse but found he could not. A man who commanded dozens of other men upon the most dangerous surface on earth, and he could not now command his own heartbeats.

"Patricia, did you go that morning?" he whispered. "Were you merely late?"

Silence met him.

"Tell me you went," he uttered, heart in his throat, "and that I have not been alone in regretting that I left that day after so short a time." The vulnerability in his voice was foreign to him. He could not alter it. "Tell me."

But she slept, her breathing light and even, and she told him nothing.

He turned his head and took in her beauty. Her hair spread in abandoned tangles upon the white linen, her lips closed now, soft and pink, lashes and lids draped over the cornflowers he had never forgotten.

"I was a coward." He spoke quietly. "By your speech, your dress, your very being, I knew I did not deserve you and I feared you recognized that. I feared you would not come, and I was too afraid to remain as the minutes passed, to see that proven true." He stroked her cheek, her skin silken and warm. "If I had not left when I did, I might have waited there for you forever, Patricia Ramsay."

She stirred, releasing a soft sigh, and turned her face into his palm.

"Did you love your husband, my beautiful, passionate Isolde?" he whispered. "Tell me he did not repay your love with coldness, and I will be content for the years I lost to him." He held his breath. "Did you love him?"

The sweet smile traced her lips once more, wistful as though in dreaming. "I loved you."

Nik did not sleep. He spent the remaining hours of the night composing a speech in his head. In truth he had been composing it for nine years. By the time black gave way to gray in the sky without, he was prepared. He could not give her a title but if she wished to retain the baronet's, he would not deny her that. He could, however, give her wealth, and a heart thoroughly hers since that day nine years ago.

But when she stirred and her cornflower eyes opened sleepily into the pale dawn light, then she stretched like a kitten and offered him her enticing smile, he lost sufficient rational mind to give his speech. He kissed her, she touched him, and instead he gave her pleasure again.

After, when she slipped back into sleep, he arose and went to his bedchamber and dressed. Her scent lingered upon his skin and he nearly returned to her. He restrained himself, going instead to the taproom to command coffee and the settlement of the bill. Rum shuffled in and tugged his cap.

"Be setting off this morning, Cap'n?"

"We will accompany Lady Morgan's party to their destination. Instruct Mr. Carr to prepare the carriage."

Rum gave him a shrewd look. "Coming on the fifteenth tomorrows, sir."

"I had no idea you could read so well, Rum. I am impressed. Less impressed, of course, that you seem to be reading my correspondence." He allowed himself a slight grin.

Rum scowled, his weathered face puckering. "T'aint right, a sailor not going after treasure."

"We've time still." But Nik had already found his treasure. His friend Jag's would have to wait.

Through the taproom window a carriage appeared clattering into the yard. Its yellow-rimmed wheels and black, crested panels were encrusted with mud, the four showy animals in the traces likewise spattered. A gentleman and a lady climbed from it and moments later entered the taproom. Nik bowed. The gentleman nodded.

He returned to his coffee.

"Sir?"

He swiveled about, brow lifted.

"I beg your pardon," the gentleman drawled. "My lady wishes me to inquire of you whether a party of three ladies resides within this inn?" His cool gaze swept up and down Nik with entitled ease. "You seem a gentleman and so I have not hesitated to ask. Anything to avoid commerce with an innkeeper, I say."

Aside from the round, sand-colored dog cradled in her arms, the lady was a study in angles, with drawn skin that proclaimed her mature years. But the features could not be mistaken, pale, protruding eyes and long nose. Without doubt, Miss Haye's sister.

"There is such a party in residence here," Nik replied. "I have recently assisted them with a mishap with their carriage."

The lady sniffed. "Never mind that. Lord Perth and I have now arrived and you are released from your assistance to my daughter-in-law's party."

It was a dismissal, plain and clear.

"It was my honor."

"Undoubtedly." The gentleman glanced about the room, taking in a pair of laborers at a far table, and curled his lip.

Nik schooled his features to a shipmaster's diplomatic impassivity. "Madam, allow me to introduce myself. I am Nikolas Acton. You are perhaps the Dowager Lady Morgan?"

She looked down her narrow nose at him, an impressive feat for a diminutive lady to accomplish with a man of his height.

"I am."

"And you, my lord—" He should not ask, for rather more reasons than the appalling show of bad manners it represented. "How might you be connected to this charming family?"

"I am Lady Morgan's fiancé, of course."

CHAPTER NINE

Patricia awoke to absolute, perfect, delicious languor. She stretched out her toes, then her fingers, then her legs and arms and her entire body. Warm beneath the covers, she could see the fire fading to embers in the grate. He had lit it after making love to her a second time. A smile crept across her lips.

It expanded.

Then it burst into delirious joy.

She sat up, strewing the covers around her, and took in clean, glorious lungfuls of air. He *must* love her. No man could make love to a woman like that without strong feeling.

She hoped.

She leapt out of the bed in which he had brought her to ecstasy many times, and did a little pirouette. She felt like a girl again, but this time absolutely free. No more bowing to her mother-in-law's wishes, or even to Oliver's. If Oliver had wanted her to know something important, he should have told her before he died. She had better things to do than go running around after secret messages.

Better things to do?

A better *man* to do.

She slapped her palms against her cheeks and dissolved into laughter.

Calanthia burst into the room. "Tricky, you—"

Patricia grabbed up her shift off the floor and threw it over her head.

"What on earth are you doing standing in the middle of your room completely naked?"

"Mm. Bathing?" She could not wipe the silly smile from her face.

Callie's brow creased. "Well that is neither here nor there." She set her fists on her hips. "What did you do to poor Captain Acton?"

"Do?" Rather, he had done most of it to her. But she very much hoped he would teach her how to reciprocate soon.

"Yes, *do*. For I can only imagine you sent him away, which is positively criminal when anybody can see that he is smitten with you. For pity's sake, he asked me if you are in love with Lord Perth."

Her pulse sped, cold dread grabbing her.

"Is he gone?"

"At least half an hour since."

"I did not send him away. I did not even speak with him this morning." Not since dawn when he had taken her in his arms again and given her fierce, tender pleasure that had left her calling his name repeatedly against his shoulder. "Why would he ask about Lord Perth? And what did you say?"

"I said of course you are not!"

Patricia sank to her bed. He had left. Oh, God, *he had left*, after making love to her like that. But he had given her precisely what she asked for—a single night. And now it was just as nine years ago and her heart must be broken in silence again. She wanted to curl up in a ball and cry forever.

Calanthia shook her head. "Tricky, you are an ass."

She choked back tears. "Callie, I cannot—"

"No. I will not refrain from using the wonderfully apt language Maggie has taught me. If you cannot see it you must be blind. He looks at you like the men of our family look at their pointer bitches. You are simply too much of a sapskull to see it, traipsing about as though widowhood were something to be desired rather than corrected."

"I do not wish to remain a widow." She wished quite desperately to be Mrs. Nikolas Acton. But that, it seemed, was not to be. How could he have left her *again*?

"You behave as though you do." Calanthia's brow came down. "I don't know why you have been holding yourself aloof from every gentleman who comes to call. You are not wearing the willow for Oliver. But— and I cannot believe I am about to speak words alarmingly like the dowager's— but your sons deserve a father and you deserve a husband. Captain Acton is perfectly breathtaking, a famous war hero, and charming, and you are a fool if you think gentlemen like that appear upon one's doorstep every day. A girl would be lucky if such a man came along even once in a lifetime." She relaxed her stance. "There, I have had my say."

"I appreciate your concern for the boys." Her words lumbered over the lump in her throat. "But you must be mistaken about Captain Acton." Wretchedly mistaken. Perhaps she should have told him everything. She had dreamed telling him she loved him, and it had been the sweetest fantasy.

But . . . ?

"Callie, why did he ask you about Lord Perth?"

"Because the dullard is here! The dowager too." She flopped down into a chair. "It is the most horrid ending to a lovely holiday that I have ever experienced."

"They are here? Whatever for?"

"She got a notion into her head from something Auntie Elsbeth suggested in London, that you went off on this trip to find a new father for the boys. She has brought Lord Perth to finally make you an offer. You won't accept him. Oh, say you will not!"

"Of course not." She went to her traveling case. "I must go down." She pulled on a gown.

"Tricky, you have forgotten your stays. And petticoat."

"Button me, will you?"

"But—"

"If you do not button me I shall go down like this."

Five minutes later, her hair hastily knotted, wearing no stockings or stays, with circles beneath her eyes and a pain of loss in her heart so powerful she could barely draw breath, she met Oliver's mother and her suitor in the parlor.

"Good morning, daughter." The dowager's gaze raked her, but she put her cheek forward to be bussed.

"I will not kiss you hello, my lady. I do not particularly like you, and I do not kiss people I do not like." She turned to the sandy-haired gentleman standing by the hearth, dressed to the nines in shining boots and high collars. The contrast between his haughty astonishment and Nik's sparkling smile would have been comical if her heart weren't breaking. "And I am never, ever going to kiss you, my lord." Tears trembled at the back of her throat. "I wish you will both leave now."

"Patricia! How dare you speak to me in such a manner, and to Lord Perth who has come this distance to condescend to you?"

"You are not my mother any longer, Lady Morgan, and I really don't see the need to pretend you are. As for Lord Perth, I believe I have made it clear enough with my indifference to him upon numerous occasions that I am not desirous of his suit, although I am not unaware of the honor he does me. Now, if you will excuse me, I must dress." She turned.

"You ungrateful girl!" trailed into the foyer behind her, but Patricia did not care. She had lost the man she loved, *again*. Now the only thing she had left was life to live, this time according to her own choices.

"What happens now?" Callie's eyes were bright.

"We finish our journey." She may as well conclude matters with Oliver once and for all before moving on with her life, and he had sent her on this journey for their sons' sake apparently. The ache inside her was violent. But at least she had one night with Nik, one perfect night in which she had lived with passion.

Calanthia touched her arm. "Tricky, I admire you. Your courage. It is so . . . real."

She managed a weak smile. "Oh, do not admire me. I learned it all from a young man I met years ago and have never stopped dreaming of since."

The road was mired muck beneath his horse's hooves and Nik was taking it in the wrong direction.

He did not want to leave her. But his mind and body rebelled against his heart, saddling his horse and riding off, every word his father and brothers had ever uttered of his worthlessness clamoring in his ears. Forcefully his heart reminded his head that he had faced down ships with double his cannonry, blown a hole in a French blockade a mile long, and bent his bow into wind that could tear canvas from spars. He was a goddamned war hero! But the voices in his head insisted that all amounted to nothing, and his horse continued to carry him away from the woman he loved who once again had told him she wanted him while poised to marry another man.

A cluster of buildings appeared in the mists ahead and he rode into the posting house yard. His horse needed the rest, but he needed her.

"Why, Captain Acton. What a delightful surprise!"

He turned to the trilling voice emerging from the building. He recognized the woman's fluttering smile and prominent nose.

He bowed. "Good day, Mrs. Chapel."

"Acton?" A gentleman paused at the threshold, Miss Chapel upon his arm. "Captain Nikolas Acton?"

"I am afraid you have the advantage of me, sir."

The man chuckled. "No doubt you believe so. It was quite a night, that night in Lisbon. With the quantity of Port we consumed, I am frankly surprised I recall it myself." He nodded to the ladies. "Pray forgive my candid speech, cousins. Wartime makes men apt to drink to excess and do foolish things. Doesn't it, Acton? Why, I believe at one point that night we were even comparing battle scars." He chuckled and came forward to clasp Nik's hand. "George Chapel. Fine to see you again."

"Captain Acton," Miss Chapel said, fixing him with a direct look, "you have not yet thrown off your doldrums, I see."

"My dear Tansy!" her mother tittered. "What will you say next?"

"He is terribly sad, Mama. Anyone can see that if they look beneath the handsome surface."

"Oh, dear." Mrs. Chapel waved her kerchief about her flushed face. "What am I to do with her? She fancies herself an artist."

"But he is a naval officer and you were in the army, George," Miss Chapel said. "How did you meet?"

"We shared a mutual acquaintance. Have you seen Grace lately, Acton, or is he still on the Continent?"

"I believe he has been in Paris for some time." Nik was not interested in war reminiscences, only in retracing his steps. In eight years upon the sea he had learned to fight. Like Grace and Chapel, he had thrown himself into the fray for England. Now, like he had won every battle he ever entered, he would win her. And if by the time he reached the inn she was no longer there, he would find her. This time he knew her name.

His breaths stilled.

Good God.

He pivoted to the horses. "Rum, where is the letter?"

His steward tugged an envelope from his coat pocket. Nik snatched Jag's missive and tore it open.

"Acton?" Chapel said. "Is everything quite all right?"

He scanned the page.

A companion of my early years on the Peninsula—a gentleman I believe you met upon one of your brief sojourns on land with us—discovered a treasure of great worth.

Nik's hands shook. "Chapel, who drank with us that night in Lisbon, other than John Grace?"

Chapel's brows went up. "Babcocke and Sams, two of Britain's finest."

"Anyone else?"

"Well, you seafaring boys, of course."

Nik's shoulders fell. "No other army officers?"

Chapel shrugged. "Morgan was there, of course. But he barely touched a drop so I cannot say he drank with us." He cast an apologetic grin at Miss Chapel. "One shouldn't speak ill of the dead, but I never did care for Oliver Morgan. A soldier needs to loosen his cravat every once in a while, but that fellow was far too stiff."

Nik's heart thundered. In all the years since those months when he had searched for Patricia, he had only spoken of her to one man. A man he met and drank with one cold winter night on the Peninsula, who once he'd heard the beginning of Nik's story encouraged him to continue it. In detail.

A man whose name until this moment he had forgotten.

Rather, he had made himself forget.

He'd been thoroughly disguised, and perhaps even at the time he knew Morgan was not. In a drunken monologue he had told him everything, from the color of her hair to their appointment to meet at the Maypole the following morning. Wallowing in his regret, he had looked up from his empty glass to Morgan's pale, cool eyes and the man's only words were, "Perhaps if you had waited longer that morning, you would not have lost her."

"Come to think of it," Chapel said in an odd voice, "after that night Morgan seemed peculiarly interested in you. He pestered Jag with any number of questions about your people and what not. Once when we were passing through a port I even heard him speaking with common sailors about you." He chuckled. "Jealousy, no doubt. Not every fellow can be a war hero and a handsome devil too." He smiled down at Miss Chapel.

Nik dropped his gaze to the letter in his unsteady hands.

The treasure will not remain long in its present location . . . In short, it could easily be lost.

Coincidence, be damned. He would not lose this treasure. Never again.

"Forgive me, Chapel. Ladies." He bowed and cut for his horse.

"Acton? Are you well, old chap?"

"Captain Acton, where are you going?"

He swung atop his mount and pulled it around. "To a May Day festival."

The cousins greeted Patricia, Calanthia, and Oliver's aunt with embraces and fond kisses. Patricia sank into their warmth, welcoming the women's fawning attention for the distraction it provided. Even when the gentlemen seized opportunity to turn conversation to dogs and hunting she was grateful. But she found she could not wish away her feelings, as she had not been able nine years ago in this same house. She escaped to the garden, all brown and wet beneath the late-winter sun, where her aunt found her.

"Dear me, you mustn't fritter the afternoon away here." She smiled vaguely. "Not when Oliver's letter specifically indicated you must go to the festival grounds."

Patricia's eyes popped wide. "How do you know of Oliver's letter? But it never said such a thing!"

"I daresay your letter was different from mine, the dear boy. He always wished to please his old aunt." Her eyes grew mistier.

Patricia grasped her hand. "Aunt, I pray you, explain this to me. Did my husband send you a letter as well?"

"Years ago." A tear teetered upon the rim of her protruding eye. Patricia's pulse raced.

"May I see it?"

"Oh, no, no. He would not care for that. He never liked anyone else to know he confided in me, especially not his mother. Poor boy was terrified of her, after all."

"Terrified? Aunt Elsbeth, please tell me what you know!"

She patted Patricia's hand. "Go to the Maypole, dear. Oliver buried a treasure there for you."

Patricia kissed her aunt's hands. "Thank you. I do not know precisely why, but thank you!" She dashed for the house. Calanthia discovered her donning her cloak in the foyer.

"Where are you going?"

"Out." She grabbed her bonnet and ran through the doorway, her sister in pursuit.

In the stable the old groom peered into her fraught face and chewed upon his lip.

"Maypole again, hm?"

"You remember?"

"Not likely to forget that one, miss." His mouth screwed into a grin. "I'll drive. Time I see what all the fuss is about."

The three miles seemed to last a lifetime, the sun dipping steadily toward the horizon. They rounded the final bend to the village and fifty yards in the clear distance stood the lone Maypole, a sturdy tree trunk buried in the earth. As on that morning nine years ago, the field around it was completely empty.

Her gaze darted to the wooden fence of the competition sheep pasture. No animals inhabited the pens now, only the pale green of new grass.

But she could not give up hope.

"My aunt said I must dig at the Maypole for something buried there."

"Auntie said *what*?"

"Didn't bring a shovel along, miss."

Patricia looked about. "There! A cottager's hut."

"Don't know how them villagers'll like digging around the Maypole. Hundred years old if it's a day."

But Patricia was already jumping from the carriage. "A little hole won't hurt it." She ran across the green toward the hut.

Callie followed. "Tricky, what *is* this all about?"

She reached the hut and pounded on the door. A heavy-set woman answered, wiping floury hands upon an apron. "Can I help you, miss?"

"Good day. Have you a shovel I can borrow?"

"Now, what would a lady want a shovel for?"

"To dig up a parcel my late husband left in the ground for me."

"If she wants a shovel, Mother," a portly man said from

behind the woman, his whiskered jowls jiggling, "there's no sense in not giving it to her." He sized her up. "But you'll be needing a man to do the digging. You're nothing but a reed, if you don't mind me saying."

"Not at all. And I shall pay you."

"Keep your silver." He moved his wife aside and came out the door, then went to a shed beside the hut for the shovel. "Where did he bury it?"

"Beneath the Maypole."

His heavy brow lowered. "Maypole's sacred around here."

She clutched her hands together. "Please, sir? This is— This is life to me."

"Constable better'd not see me at it. Be run out of the district. But let's go."

"Thank you!"

They marched across the green, Patricia and the cottager followed by his wife, Callie, and the old groom. A scruffy boy pulling a goat on a lead crossed their path and straggled along.

The pole rose at least eighteen feet straight from the grassy earth. In a month and a half it would again be crowned with a wreath and twined with gaily colored ribbons, and the local maidens would dance. She studied the ground beneath it.

"He buried it at least four years ago."

"Best to get started 'fore it comes on to dark." The cottager set the shovel to the earth, slammed his heel onto it, and brought up a clod of grassy soil. Then another, and another.

Patricia held her breath.

The goat boy scratched his thatch of hair. "What's he diggin' for?"

"Dead husband's treasure," the cottager's wife said sotto

voce. "I'll tell you, if he left me something it'd better be above ground."

"It's got to do with the festival some years back," the groom muttered.

"But this wasn't in the letter, Tricky. How do you know to—"

The shovel clanked against metal.

"Well, I'll be Old Father Christmas," the cottager uttered.

"Yes." Patricia's voice cracked.

A few more shovelfuls of soil came up and, stripping off her gloves, she fell to her knees. Her fingers sought the edges of the box, the size of a large book, and pried it free from the earth.

"Ma'am?" The cottager's wife proffered Patricia the apron and she wiped the box clean. It was fastened with only a tab closure. With shaking fingers, she lifted the lid. In a wrapper of red felt lay a small leather-bound volume. It slipped into her muddied palms and a sob caught in her throat.

"What is it?" Callie whispered.

"My diary. I threw it away years ago. I threw it right into the grate. It burned." Only the edges were singed, though, the back cover cracked from the fire's heat.

"Why did you wish to burn your diary?"

Because it told the story of a young man she met the day before she learned of her betrothal. It detailed that day, and the days, weeks and months that followed during which she wept over losing him while she struggled to become accustomed to a husband who, no matter how she tried, gave her only the admiration one might offer a fine statue or painting—not a living breathing woman aching for warmth and laughter.

"I threw it away because I had given up hope." Her fingers

traced the crusty edges of the binding.

"Did he read it, mum?"

"Man don't read his wife's diary, boy."

"Well he buried it here then told her to come find it! Just saying p'raps he read it first."

"He did." In it, clearly, he had learned of the appointment at the Maypole.

"Here there!" a firm voice came across the green, and more distant, hoof beats. "What's going on there?"

"Constable," the cottager said in a resigned voice.

"Churchwarden too," the groom muttered.

"We'll never hear the end of it now." The cottager's wife sighed.

"I will speak with them." Calanthia sounded twice her age. "My brother is a viscount."

The others moved away, but Patricia barely noticed. She opened the cover of the diary and her husband's script stared up at her. Her heart raced. She unfolded the single sheet of foolscap.

16 August 1809

Patricia,

    I knew when we wed that you did not love me. But I was a fool to believe that simply because I could not engage your affections, another man would not—had not already.

    I am angry now. I imagine myself betrayed and deceived. A man of extreme passions, however, I am not. I did not wish to cause you pain in taking you as my wife, and I blame you for your unhappiness as much as myself. I would like to imagine this interlude of yours a childish whim and that by now you have forgotten it entirely. But I know you perhaps better than you understand. Your heart is constant. I cannot force you to love me, but so too I cannot release you. If I had known upon that day of our betrothal what I know now, I would not have released you even then.

    I bury this here in the hope that some day I will find the courage to tell you that I understand, or—in greater hope—to allow it to rot into forgotten memory. To have brought it here to dispose of in this manner is a gesture of symbolic nonsense. But for two years already you have made me a fool for you. And although I have never been able to express it to you as you wish, a fool for you I will remain to the day I die.

       Oliver

Tears tumbled over the rims of Patricia's eyes and onto the page.

"Tricky?" Her sister's voice came beneath the pounding of horses' hooves. "Tricky!"

She dashed the tears off her cheeks and looked over her shoulder. The villagers and groom and her sister were all turned toward a pair of horsemen advancing at a gallop.

The bottom fell out of her heart. She stood on shaking legs as Nik pulled his mount to a skidding halt and jumped from the saddle.

"Do you know why I wear this ring?" She thrust out her hand as she walked to him and he to her, swiftly. "I wear it because the girl for whom it was intended perished before she could enjoy life with the man she adored. And for nine years I have felt as though I did too. For one miraculous day I lived, and then you disappeared and I lost that. Instead I wore all the passion bottled up inside me in this silly ring, believing I could not have it in my real life because it did not belong there."

He reached her and pulled her into his arms. His hand came around her face and his thumb stroked across her cheek, his beautiful eyes scanning her features full of awe.

"That is why I asked you to make love to me yesterday," she said brokenly. "I wanted to feel that again, even if only for a moment, so that I might have something to carry with me through the next nine years. The next ninety. But I don't want that any longer. I want it always. I want to feel the laughter and excitement and passion I feel with you every day of my life." She pulled in a deep breath. "What are you doing here?"

"A very fine speech, Lady Morgan." He smiled slightly, but his voice was not entirely even. "Long, but quite good. I liked it."

"Will you cease teasing me!" She pressed her fist to his chest. "Why are you here?"

"To ask you if you came here that morning."

She lifted the diary. "Feel free to read it all yourself. My husband did, apparently."

He glanced at the diary, his breaths hard, then back at her. "Patricia, did you come?"

"Of course I did! But my father and mother took it upon themselves that very morning to betroth me to a man I barely knew without my consent. I was late, only, and you were not here."

His eyes shone. "No coincidences." He bent his head and

captured her mouth in a full kiss of need and strength and sheer beauty. She clung to him and a sob escaped her that he caught and transformed into a sigh. She did not want it to end, the caress of his mouth that made her tremble in love. But he separated their lips and pressed his brow to hers.

"I searched for you for a year."

She stilled. "You—?" Her throat closed. His gaze adored her so openly, showing her his feelings. She finally uttered, "A year?"

"I fell in love with you. I wanted you beyond reason. No matter how I told myself I was a fool—for you had not come—I could not stop searching. I went to war to force an end to my desperate search."

"You came here that morning?"

"I came, and I despaired. Even not knowing who you were, I knew I was not good enough for you. I knew that with time overnight to reconsider, you had realized that. But I could not give you up."

"I did not reconsider. I should have refused them, but I had never disobeyed them, and you had not come. Still, I never ceased regretting it."

"We were both mistaken," he said tenderly and kissed the tip of her nose, then her brow, then her cheeks, his arms tightening about her like in a dream, but no longer a dream. This was finally reality.

"If I had not married Oliver," she whispered, "I would not have my sons. And you would not have become a great war hero."

"Patricia, I will care for your sons and protect them as though they were my own. I could not do otherwise."

Tears gathered behind her eyes anew. "You are a good man, Nik. A great man."

"I became who I am for you." He grasped her hands. "If we had met that morning, it's true, I might not have thrown myself into battles with such enthusiasm. But I would have become a ship captain as you ordered. I would have done whatever required to win you. I think something within me believed that if I pursued that course, I would someday find you again."

"But when you did find me, you teased, even when you believed me married. And why did you leave here so abruptly this morning?"

"Ignoble reasons. Anger. Hurt. Jealousy."

"But no longer?"

"No longer." He stroked the backs of his fingers along her cheek. "Patricia, your husband sent me here."

She gasped.

His eyes sparkled. "I knew him. One night with him in Portugal, I told him about the girl I had lost. Until two hours ago I had forgotten his name. But he did not forget mine, and for that I thank him eternally."

Holding her hands tight, he went to his knee before her as he had on that day long ago.

"What's he doing down there in the mud?"

"Proposing, lad. Gen'lemen don't care about their trousers."

"Always got a spare, I s'pose."

Nik kissed her hands softly, soberly. "Patricia Ramsay Morgan, marry me. I don't care if you are betrothed to a hundred titled Midases successively. I will fight every one of them before giving you up again. Through rain, snow, wind, and high water I will remain here at this fool pole until you say yes."

Laughter tumbled through her tears. "Yes."

"Yes," he said in wonderment. "Yes." He stood, drew her into his arms again, and kissed her. Applause erupted around them, hearty huzzahs, and Calanthia's joyful laughter. But Patricia heard only the beating of Nik's heart entwined with her own, and the intoxicating rush of life's passionate embrace.

In the breakfast parlor of his elegant Mayfair townhouse, the Earl of Savege took up a cup of coffee and *The Times*. Crossing long, muscular legs to which at least half a dozen beautiful married ladies had written poems, not to mention any number of exquisite young widows, he leaned back in his chair.

The gossip column on the right proclaimed the imminent wedding of Captain Nikolas Acton of the Royal Navy to Lady Patricia Morgan. The happy couple would reside in London, with no present plans for the war hero to return to sea. Under the heading *Board of the Admiralty*, the facing page announced that a search would soon be undertaken for the notorious pirate Redstone. Several vessels on light duty since the Treaty of Paris would be enlisted to hunt down the criminal for trial and execution.

Alex drew a slow breath. A light, cool breeze blew in through the cracked parlor window, scented with coal dust, pavement, and rain. London at its late-winter best.

And yet, two hundred miles to the west, the wind blew fresh with salt off the ocean mingled with the mossy green scent of the Devonshire hills. But Alex could not go to his estate there quite yet, no matter how he longed for it. Spring was fast advancing and his ship and crew already awaited him. If the Navy had finally determined to come for Redstone, then Redstone had better be at sea when those boys started looking. A man must keep up appearances, after all, even if that appearance was a complete falsity.

He glanced again at the gossip column, a slight grin tracing a mouth that had given pleasure to more women than the *ton* could count.

His old friend had chosen a woman over the sea. Better this way. Alex would not be obliged to blow Nik's ship to pieces if he were to find him. It was a shame though, the petticoat ensnarement of a fighting man. But some men were deuced fools for the fairer sex. Even heroes.

AUTHOR'S NOTE

In pursuit of unexceptionably noble ends, the heroes of my *Rogues of the Sea* trilogy nevertheless occasionally find themselves working at cross-purposes to the Royal Navy. So it was great fun to turn over the coin and write Nik, a sailor who became a hero through serving his kingdom's military. I dedicate this story to the brave men and women of our armed services whose ultimate hope is peace for all.

My profoundest thanks for assistance go to Margaret Brill, Georgann Brophy, Georgie Cashin, Laurent Dubois, Melinda Leigh, and Marquita Valentine.

Keep reading for

a sneak peek at

Captured by a Rogue Lord

On sale April 2011

> *Many were the men whose cities he saw*
> *and whose minds he learned, and many*
> *the woes he suffered in his heart upon*
> *the sea, seeking to win his own life.*

> —HOMER, *Odyssey*

"Gorblimey, Cap'n Redstone. Cut off his head already."

With his long, leather-clad legs braced upon the pitch-sealed deck, Alexander "Redstone" Savege stared down at the cowering form, his broad-brimmed hat casting a shadow over the figure. The whelp's skinny arms encircled his head, his pallor grayish from a dredge in frigid coastal waters. He wasn't more than fourteen if he were a day. Far too young to be living such a wretched life.

Alex rubbed his callused palm across his face, sucking in briny air laced with the scent of oncoming rain, his gray eyes shadowed. He gripped the hilt of his cutlass, a thick, inelegant weapon, long as his arm and meant for only one purpose—the same as the ten iron guns and pair of agile pivots jutting from the *Cavalier*'s sleek sides, all at rest now but easily primed for battle.

Violence, the hell's ransom of a pirate. Once mother's milk to Alex, now a curse.

He cast a glance at his helmsman, a hulking, chestnut-skinned beast sporting a missing earlobe and a leering smile. Big Mattie was always eager to see blood spilt. The faces of the five dozen sailors clustered around showed the same gleeful anticipation.

Alex withheld a sigh. He'd brought this on himself. The lot of them knew, after all, the swift ease with which their master's blade could fly.

"Pop his cork right off, Cap'n," cackled a sexagenarian with cheeks of uncured leather. "Or slice his nose and ears."

"Stick 'im in the ribs, just like you did to that Frenchie wi' the twenty-gun barque we sunk in 'thirteen," an ebony sailor chimed in.

Alex repressed a grimace, his hand tightening around the sword handle. He fixed the grommet with a hard glare.

"Are you ready to die for your crime, Billy?" he grumbled in his deepest, scratchiest voice, the sort that never saw the inside of a St. James's gentlemen's club or a beautiful lady's Mayfair bedchamber. The sort that his mother, sister, and most of his acquaintances would be shocked to know he could affect.

The Seventh Earl of Savege never cussed, rarely swore, and only in the direst circumstances raised his voice above an urbane murmur. Handy with his fives, expert with saber, épée, and pistol alike, he never employed any of them, to the eternal vexation of not a few cuckolded husbands. He preferred per-fumed boudoirs to malodorous boxing cages, and the elegant peace and quiet of a fine gaming establishment to the dust and discomfort of a carriage race.

But each time Alex stepped aboard the *Cavalier*, he left the Earl of Savege behind.

"Blast and damn, Bill, are you trying to fob off a whisker?" He glowered. Several of his crew members echoed his discontent with mumbles.

"I didn't cackle, Cap'n. I swears it," the youth mewled. "You can't kill me for not telling them nothing, can you?"

Alex took a long breath, steadying the blood pounding through his veins, fueled by a dangerous cocktail of anger, frustration, and pure cerebral fatigue.

"I can kill you for soiling my ears with that sound," he grunted. "What's that coming from your throat, a plea or a girl's whimper?" He tapped his sword tip to the boy's bony rear and nudged. "Stand up and let me hear if you can speak like a man instead."

The lad climbed to his feet.

"On my mother's grave, Cap'n, I didn't tell any of them smugglers about our covey. I didn't."

"Your mother is still alive, Billy, and happy you've nothing to do with her any longer, I'll merit." Alex sheathed his sword.

The whelp's eyes went wide. "Then you ain't going to kill me after all?"

"Not today, but you'll scrub the decks for a fortnight," Alex growled. "And caulk that crack on the gun deck at the bowsprit. Caulk the whole damn deck, for that matter. The rest of you get back to work."

Nothing stirred atop but the fluttering banner, gold rapier upon black undulating in the fresh breeze.

"Now!" Alex bellowed.

Billy jumped, and the crew scattered like grapeshot. Alex moved toward the stair to belowdecks. Big Mattie lingered.

"You ain't gonna even strap him to the capstan for a day, Cap'n?" he prodded. "But he gave up our covey to those curs at the tavern in the village. Got to make an example of him. What do you want, for the rest of these lilies"—he gestured around the ship—"to go spouting their mouths off?"

"Stubble it, Mattie, or I'll stubble it for you," Alex warned without breaking stride, hand still upon the metal at his hip. He forbore grinding his straight, white teeth, the only bright spot on his polish-blackened face except the whites of his eyes.

"Big Mattie has a point, Captain," his quartermaster said quietly, falling in beside him, matching him stride for stride. Jinan stood a mere inch shy of Alex's considerable height, of similar build though somewhat leaner in the chest, like his Egyptian ancestors.

Alex met Jin's steady blue gaze, the intelligence glinting in it reminding him as always why he left his ship in this man's hands for most of the year.

"Big Mattie has an unhealthy thirst for blood, like his master," he muttered, swinging down the steep steps to the gun deck, leaving the gray of the spring day behind. "We don't need to worry about the smugglers. They'll keep to their own if we keep to ours." From habit his gaze scanned the cannons before he ducked beneath the beams.

They entered the day chamber, appointed in Aubusson carpets, with brocaded upholstery sheathed in walnut, cherry-wood furniture, and a crystal carafe cradling French brandy on the sideboard. A silver and onyx writing set graced the desktop in the adjacent office, and ivory bookends supported leather-bound volumes of Greek verse. Along with the bedchamber opposite, and the finest linens, it looked like the private rooms of a lord of the realm. Unbeknownst to all aboard except Alex and his quartermaster, they were.

Jin closed the door and affixed the shutters of the windows letting onto the deck. He folded his arms.

"Thirst for blood, my arse. Mattie might gripe, but your mercy stands you in good stead with the men, as always. Even when they're itching to be ashore."

"Lilies, the lot of them, just like he said." Alex waved a dismissive hand. "They ought to be ashamed to be weary of the sea after a mere seven weeks abroad."

"They're not weary, merely looking forward to a lick at the grog we took off that Barbadian trader." Jin shook his head. "You're right about the smugglers, of course. But, Alex, the hull won't clean itself. We've got to careen the ship."

"Which you should have done before the last cruise."

"I couldn't heave to for that. Not after the *Etoile* challenged us off Calais."

"And left you twiddling the sweeps when the wind died and she failed to show for the fight. Jin, I did not give you permission to go after that blasted privateer. We are at peace with France now, or hadn't you noticed? Even if we weren't, that is not our purpose."

"The men think it is, at least since you put French merchantmen off limits after the treaty last November."

"You sound as though you agree with them." Alex moved into his washroom, pulled off his sash strung with dagger and pistol along with his leather waistcoat, and hung them upon a hook. His sweat-stained linen shirt came next. "Have you finally become greedy for pirate's gold after all these years, my friend?" He drew on a fresh garment.

Jin scowled, marring the aristocratic lines of a face that mingled the blood of English nobles and eastern princes.

"Don't insult me. But after our run-in with that American frigate last week and the quick repairs, the crew deserves a break." He paused. "And so do you."

"Have a yen to take the summer cruise without me? Are you hoping to storm the Channel and win a fat French prize despite my prohibition?" Alex chose a dark, simply tailored coat from his compact wardrobe and took up a wrinkled cravat. Tubbs would have his head for donning such a rag. But he didn't answer to his valet, or to anyone else.

"Of course not," Jin replied. "If you say we mayn't take merchantmen any longer, we will not. The men got accustomed to it after three successful years, though."

"The war did not last long enough for some."

"Long enough for you to take out a half-dozen French men-of-war," Jin murmured.

Alex ignored his friend's look of measured admiration and wound the linen about his neck. It smelled of salted fish, but that was a good sight better than plenty of the other aromas on the *Cavalier* at the end of the seven-week cruise. Jin was right. Both ship and crew needed a break before the next trip out. And, according to the note Billy brought back from his trip ashore last night, he had business at home.

He wrapped the cravat about his jaw, stretching it over his nose and tucking it fast at the base of his skull. With the black face paint and a concealing hat, the disguise had not failed him in eight years. It still astounded him, despite the *Cava-*

lier's repeated visits to the north Devon coast of late, that no one among the *bon ton* had connected the notorious buccaneer Redstone with the seventh Earl of Savege. With a vast, prosperous estate stretching across miles of remote Devonshire coastline, the earl was far too busy in London whoring and gambling away his fortune to set foot at home often.

Alex took some pride in Redstone's mysterious identity. His brother, Aaron, positively delighted in it. Blast him.

"Last autumn the men grew richer than bilge rats should," Jin commented.

Alex dropped a nondescript hat atop his head and tugged it low over his brow.

"Then they should be content this season with an occasional English yacht. In the meantime, allow them ashore, north as usual. But for God's sake tell them to behave and stay clear of those blasted smugglers. I don't want them getting mixed up with that bunch of miscreants, or being mistaken for them."

"The locals know the boys well enough by now." Jin frowned. "But Billy didn't like the looks of the *Osprey*'s crew, and he brought back news." He shook his head, bracing his stance against a sudden sway of the ship. The far-reaching eddies of Bristol Channel were friendly enough in gentle weather, but rain beckoned. Alex could feel it in his blood like he felt sunset, moonrise, and the ebb of the tides.

"What have they done?"

"Seems they roughed up a girl."

His gaze snapped up. "Roughed up?"

"Aye." Jin nodded. "A group of them."

"What girl?"

"A dairy maid. Did it right under her brothers' noses. In a

barn."

"They took a girl from a barn and no one challenged them?"

"*In* a barn—"

"No." He lifted his hand. "I understand. The farm sits upon the shore, doesn't it?" Weeks ago he'd come upon the smuggling brig out of a fog and had a good look at it. Well armed and deep in the draft, the *Osprey* was an impressive vessel. Even if she sat too far off shore for the cannon shot to reach land, sailors' muskets, cutlasses, and pikes could readily best a farmer's pitchforks and axes. The girl's brothers could not have saved her virtue, much like his own brother could not save their younger sister years earlier.

Alex headed toward the door. "Why did you wait until now to tell me this?"

"You always say you don't wish to know the business of English smugglers. Let them go their own way. But this is a nasty one. Captain goes by the name of Dunkirk."

"I don't care about the *Osprey* or her captain. Only—"

"The pleasure boats of spoilt English nobles. I know."

Alex set an even gaze upon his friend.

"If you object to the *Cavalier*'s purpose, you are free to find other employment. I have made that perfectly clear many times, and you must have enough gold stored in London banks by now to buy yourself a fleet. You owe me nothing."

Jin returned his steady stare. "I will decide when my debt to you is repaid. And you need me, now more than ever."

Alex refused to bite at that bait. He reached for the door handle.

"What about Poole, then?"

Alex paused, a hot finger of anger pressing at the base of his throat once more. But it did not spread to fill his chest as it had for so many years. Now it merely lapped at his senses, taunting him with what might have been. Revenge was sweetest served hot, and eight years had in truth cooled his thirst for blood. Now the sole reason he pursued his present course sat in solitude at Savege Park, awaiting his return.

"I will concern myself with Lord Poole when and if he ever finds us." He could wait to confront the man who, barely knowing it, had twice turned his life inside out.

"By which you mean never," Jin said casually as Alex opened the door. "He's been making very friendly with the Admiralty, if rumors can be believed. Perhaps you should spend some time sitting in your seat in Lords. Then you can ask him to his face what he intends to do about Redstone."

Alex lifted a single brow. "When you hold a peerage yourself one day, Jin, remind me not to give you foolish, unsolicited advice, will you?"

His quartermaster laughed. "See you in June?"

"I will send word. Until then, keep them out of trouble. I don't want to hear any stories of the crew getting up to rigs in the villages. My ship deserves it, if not its master."

"Aye aye, sir. I will take good care of her. And you take care of those other ladies you're abandoning this one for."

Alex grinned, his chest loosening. He left the cabin and climbed onto the main deck. Fore and aft the schooner stretched sleek and sparkling, in top order. A 135-ton, twelve-gun beauty, she was one of the fastest ships in the Atlantic. In the eight years since he'd purchased her gleaming new at St. Eustatius, then four years later sailed north into the English Channel, no one had come close to finding her. Only two ships—the American *Wasp* and the free-agent *Blackhawk*—had outrun her.

Alex had no worries that the Earl of Poole's hunters would track him down. The *Cavalier* lived much like its master, present one day, gone the next. The devil himself threw up his hands at the farcical journey into mingled heaven and hell Alex took every spring and summer for weeks upon end.

He loved the sea, its breadth and depth, scent and texture. He needn't be a blasted pirate to partake of it. But as much as he envisioned a different sort of enjoyment of the ocean, he could not give up Redstone. Not yet.

Propped at the helm, Big Mattie threw him a surly farewell, all bluster. Below, a skiff bobbed upon the green water, sailors from prow to stern with oars in hand. Alex climbed down the rope ladder and took his place in the stern. Finally he turned his gaze to the land.

The *Cavalier* had come in sight of his property the previous night, but he hadn't allowed himself to look. Now he took his fill of the coastline's narrow strips of gold sand and jutting gray rock painted with verdant moss, jewel-like beneath the sky's shuttered gaze. Beyond the coast, protected from the wind by the hill's crest, sharp, sloping fields of emerald green dotted with sheep or striped with early crops gave way to pine and elm woods and winding streams, fragrant with fresh water.

The sight met his senses like the beckoning arms of a woman, shapely, beautiful, full of promise. It was always this way. While at sea, he wished to be nowhere else. When heading toward home, he wanted nothing but his land. It was the tragic irony of his life that he spent the lion's share of every year in his Mayfair mansion.

It hadn't always been thus. Not until that night when Lambert Poole looked him dead in the bloodshot eye and assured him that they were alike as two brothers.

The skiff pulled south a league and came ashore along a modest dock Alex had built four years earlier for the purpose. In the shadow of a low cliff, overhung with stripped trees and striated rocks, a cavelike indentation provided the ideal place to shift identities. A half-mile walk inland brought him to a cottage at which his valet stored fresh linens and a change of clothing. The day still hung gray but without fog. If they'd seen the *Cavalier* from the house, Tubbs would be at the cottage waiting for him.

Alex climbed from the boat and waved off the sailors. He started up the path away from shore with nothing but a pistol and a dirk tucked in his boot, legs swiftly steadying to land. The transition never bothered him. Seven weeks at sea did not suffice to dim the sensation of walking upon solid earth. More than enough time had elapsed, however, to make him eager for his first stop when he returned to London. La Dolcetta awaited. When Alex's valet met him at the cottage door, his placid face a study in grimness, the voluptuous opera singer's boudoir seemed all the more appealing.

"What's happened, Tubbs?" Alex pulled off his hat and cravat, moving to the washstand. He accepted the soap from his manservant and scrubbed at the blacking upon his face.

"Welcome home, my lord. Your brother awaits you at the Park."

"So Billy said. You will not tell me what this is about, I suspect." Alex wiped his jaw and cheeks clean and glanced aside at his servant. Tubbs's expression remained shuttered. "No, of course not. So let us make this quick and be off."

Tubbs helped Alex dress in fresh garments suitable for his country consequence and they left the cottage. Alex's head groom already awaited them in an unmarked carriage.

"Fine to see you so soon again, my lord." Pomley tugged his cap. "Didn't know when you'd be back this time."

"It was a short cruise." Alex climbed into the seat beside the wiry old fellow and took the ribbons. Years earlier Pomley had purchased the rig and team for this use, an unremarkable carriage and unremarkable horses. Alex knew perfectly well it did not fool anyone upon his lands. Pomley and Tubbs were the only men who assisted him with his biyearly masquerade, but everyone else knew precisely who Lord Savage became each spring and summer while away from home. Not one person, from scullery maid to tenant farmer to villager, ever said a single word about it.

Occasionally, when Alex allowed himself to ponder that miracle, it awed him.

"A paying one, as always?" Pomley said with familiar ease.

Alex snapped the reins. "Relatively."

"The orphans won't go hungry this year." The groom's toothy smile broadened.

"The orphans wouldn't have gone hungry even if we had picked up only saltwater," Alex mumbled. They all thought Redstone's prize money funded the foundling hospital in Exmoor, as well as the home for sailors and soldiers' widows in Bideford. For the past four years it had. But Alex had more than enough funds to maintain those institutions for decades even without the *Cavalier*'s help.

"More satisfying this way," Pomley continued. "A right

Robin Hood do-gooder, you are, sir."

Alex stifled a cringe and glanced at Tubbs sitting behind. The valet's face was stony. Alex chuckled and whipped up the team.

Two miles along the twisting, scrubby road his house came into view. Atop an outcropping close to the coast, Savege Park arose in solitary, hulking splendor. Seat of the earldom for centuries, its construction was a mishmash of styles and purposes, built of local limestone around a medieval keep. Dotted with moss upon the leeward side, stripped by wind and rain of artifice on the windward, its gray stone walls, turrets, and terraces marked the hillcrest as though declaring to enemies, be warned, and friends be ever welcome.

Alex inhaled deeply, anticipating the fresh scent of polished wood, the smooth comfort of dry bed linens, the quiet stillness of his study.

A boy sitting atop a hillock caught sight of the carriage, leapt up and went streaking toward the house. Alex pulled to the stable gate, threw the reins to Pomley, and jumped from the box. Fifty feet took him to the front door. Why bother with further pretense when everyone now knew of his arrival?

The door opened and guilt stirred in his belly. As always.

The butler, a long line of liveried footmen and maids, and the housekeeper met him as he entered.

"It's fine to have you home, my lord." His housekeeper bobbed a curtsy, rustling starched cambric. Alex smiled at the woman who had kept his house without aid of a mistress for eight years since his father died and his mother settled in London.

"Thank you, Mrs. Tubbs. It's good to be home." He removed his long duster and hat, and his gaze traveled up the broad staircase. Leaning against the top rail, his brother cracked a mild smile.

"All hail the conquering hero." Aaron Savege's voice came lightly down into the hall, smooth yet considerably thinner than Alex's.

Everything about his twin was like that. Alex's hair and eyes were dark to Aaron's British fairness. His tall, broad frame contrasted with the slighter, slender form that lent his sibling the appearance of the churchman he ought to have been.

Alex scoffed and started up the stairs. He reached the landing and extended his hand. His brother released a vise grip upon the banister to greet him, clutching the handle of his cane with his other hand.

"Billy made it back to the ship with my note, I assume? He's a wily one. No wonder you keep him on despite his youth." Aaron turned awkwardly on the landing and in jolting steps moved toward the drawing room door.

"He carried news of all sorts," Alex replied.

Aaron cast him a glance, light brown eyes aware. "He told you about the farmer's girl?"

"And the sailors from the *Osprey*. Which family?"

"Your tenants remain unmolested. The news traveled here quickly, but I don't know the people. It was south, beyond Carlyle's land."

"Then why the urgent missive calling me to shore, little brother?"

"If you were not ready to return yet, what were you doing skulking about the Devonshire coast?"

"The hull needs scraping. I might as well come ashore here

than anywhere else."

"Ah, good. You must have taken a prize or two, then." Aaron smiled. "Who this time?"

"Two dingies worth nothing—"

"I doubt that."

"—and Effington's sloop. Tidy little boat, full of silver plate, port wine, and champagne. The crew was in alt. They're probably drinking to my lord Effington's health right now."

"And the silver will go to the orphans, no doubt. Effington? The fellow who took up with that actress after you gave the woman her *congé*. Didn't you say that he beat—"

"Yes." Alex closed the door and strode across the chamber to the sideboard. Aaron lumbered to a chair by the hearth.

"What is the pressing business you mentioned in your note that could not have waited another fortnight or two?" Alex poured a finger of brandy and swirled it in the cut crystal glass. "Has Kitty gotten into a scrape?"

"No, of course not. Last I heard from Mother, she and our sister were enjoying the season in town from the comfort of your house, as always. Gambling, also as always, but not to excess."

"Then what? Trouble with tenants? I cannot imagine anything you and Haycock together aren't able to manage without me."

"You know that's not true, Alex. He is a splendid steward. Matchless. But no one knows this estate like you do. And the people practically worship you."

"Silly fools," Alex mumbled, moving toward the window.

"You've no one to blame for it but yourself." Aaron's voice hinted at pride. "But it's not the tenants. Carlyle came over here the other day to offer his daughter's hand."

Alex turned from the sight of sloping green lawn and lifted a brow.

"To *me*?"

"Certainly not to me," his brother replied without a flicker of his even gaze. "Surprised your reputation for game and women still fails to deter hopeful parents? But, you see, you have wealth, title, and good looks to boot."

Alex ignored him. "Carlyle? Isn't his daughter firmly upon the shelf by now?"

"You know that?"

"A wise man attends to his neighbors' business, upon both sea and land."

"Forgive my impertinence." Aaron smiled, the expression lightening his habitually sober face. Alex's breath came easier for the first time since he entered the house. He grinned.

"You are forgiven." He swept a magnanimous hand through the air. "Continue."

"You have the right of it. Miss Carlyle is indeed rather long in the tooth."

"And he hopes to foist her off upon me simply because our lands march?"

"No. She isn't the daughter he offered, though she is still unmarried, I've no idea why."

"A younger sister then. Or—" He placed a palm upon his chest. "—do not say it—*elder*?"

"Because you are so discriminating when it comes to the age of a beautiful woman, of course," Aaron murmured.

"Younger, then. So the chit is beautiful?"

"Yes. Quite."

"Splendid. I shouldn't wish my countess to be an antidote."

"Will you take Carlyle's proposition to heart, then?" His brother's tone was abruptly serious.

"Why not? I might as well set up my nursery and assure the dynasty with some pretty little thing now as later." Alex's blood ran to still, unease slipping through his veins.

"What of Redstone?" his twin said slowly. "You cannot very well continue disappearing every spring and summer for weeks upon end with a wife at home."

Alex turned back to the window, wishing he stood at the rear of the house where through the glass panes the expanse of sea could be seen stretching far beyond the craggy shoreline, blue, deep, alluring.

"I have been thinking, Aaron," he ventured.

"Thinking of what, Alex?" His brother's tone revealed nothing now, damn his training for the Church.

"After the summer cruise this year I might put to shore once and for all."

Silence met him. Slowly he pivoted about upon the heel of Hoby's finest. Aaron's face was like stone.

Alex's throat tightened. "What would you think of that?" he asked with supreme nonchalance.

"You would sell the *Cavalier?* To Jinan, presumably."

"She is already his ship for most of the year."

"She is your ship, Alex, and Jin knows that better than anyone. He only remains with you because—"

"She is our ship, Aaron. Yours and mine, no matter who captains it." A dull ache settled in his chest. He struggled not to allow his gaze to slip to his brother's useless leg. "Why don't you come along on the summer cruise? It will be our last run.

We'll pick off that rogue Abernathy's yacht, as planned, and a few others I will ferret out in town this month. Maybe an old French merchantier for a finale."

"A French ship? You would not dare."

"Oh, wouldn't I?" Alex squared his shoulders. "The infamous Redstone fears neither man nor government. If they want me, let them come." He waggled his brows.

His brother's face relaxed and Alex's heart began beating again. He could not stand this, the tangled guilt, anger, and hopelessness, the searing regret that would not fade even after three years. He missed his lands and longed to linger at the Park, to walk the hills with his steward and drink a pint at the tavern with tenant farmers he'd known since he was a boy, when he was freshly returned from the West Indies with stories to tell that they listened to kindly.

But blast if his hands weren't already itching to grip the ribbons and fly to London. Remaining in his twin's company was simply too difficult.

At thirteen, Alex had learned to withstand the rigors of life upon the sea, and at twenty-three he'd chosen that life for part of each year. He could scud through a storm at ten knots, face off against a ship with twice his weight in guns, stare a musket down the barrel without flinching, and hold a blade to another man's throat with no hesitation. But when it came to what he had done to his brother, he would rather flee than face the daily reminder.

"You cannot leave the *Cavalier* behind, Alex," Aaron said quietly. "She is your true love."

Alex slanted his twin a mock-derisive look. "You think it's time I shift my affections to a human?"

"Can you?"

"Not in this lifetime, brother," Alex grunted.

Aaron dropped his gaze to his hands lying upon his lap, palms up. "You imagine me foolish to speak of love."

"Indeed I do. But I always have." Alex smiled. He must smile, ever making light of the dreams his brother had left behind when they carried him off the battlefield a broken man.

"How will you respond to Lord Carlyle?"

"Does he expect me to pay a call?"

"No. They have gone to town for her come-out."

Alex nodded. Here, fate was handing him a concrete reason to leave the country.

"What is the chit's name?"

"Charity Lucas. She is Carlyle's eldest stepdaughter."

"Lucas? Sounds familiar."

"Her brother is a baronet, young fellow, deep in the pockets. Perhaps you've seen him playing at the club. He and Carlyle are offering a mint for her dowry."

"Ah, a bride rich in both beauty and gold. For what more could I wish?"

"What more, indeed?"

An end to the charade his life had become. A wife could provide sufficient justification. A lady whose father's estate abutted his suited the purpose ideally. She would eschew town, wishing to be close to her family, and Alex would indulge her by keeping to the country more often than not. And if by chance this girl did not suit him, he might take this opportunity to find another. He knew few ladies of unblemished reputation amongst the *beau monde*, but his mother and sister would willingly oblige in that matter if he asked.

"Will you go to town immediately?"

"To make the fair maid's acquaintance and determine if we shall suit? Why not? I'll have to start scouting out our next prizes anyway." He moved toward the door. "Consider it, Aaron. One final lark before we farthel the sails for retirement. Like old times."

His brother regarded him steadily across the chamber, gentle resignation in his eyes. Alex turned about and left his twin behind.

ABOUT THE AUTHOR

ABOUT THE AUTHOR

The American Library Association's *Booklist* named Katharine Ashe one of the "New Stars of Historical Romance" and *RT Book Reviews* awarded her debut historical romance, *Swept Away By a Kiss*, a "TOP PICK!" Katharine lives in the wonderfully warm Southeast with her husband, son, two dogs, and a garden she likes to call romantic rather than unkempt. A professor of European history, she has made her home in California, Italy, France, and the northern US. Please visit her at www.katharineashe.com.

Visit www.AuthorTracker.com for exclusive information on your favorite HarperCollins authors.